Books by Sid Fleischman

HUMBUG MOUNTAIN

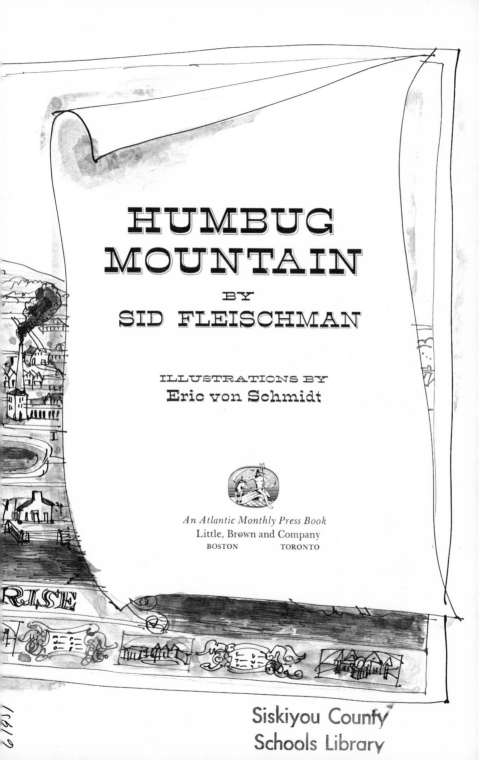

HUMBUG MOUNTAIN

BY
SID FLEISCHMAN

ILLUSTRATIONS BY
Eric von Schmidt

An Atlantic Monthly Press Book
Little, Brown and Company
BOSTON   TORONTO

FIRST EDITION

T09/78

Library of Congress Cataloging in Publication Data

Fleischman, Albert Sidney.
  Humbug Mountain.

  "An Atlantic Monthly Press book."
  SUMMARY: A young boy and his wandering family
foil villains and rout nasty varmints as they
make a home for themselves in a beached boat on
the banks of the Missouri.
  [1. The West—Fiction. 2. Humorous stories]
I. Von Schmidt, Eric. II. Title.
PZ7.F5992Hi   [Fic]   78–9419
ISBN 0–316–28569–2

ATLANTIC–LITTLE, BROWN BOOKS
ARE PUBLISHED BY
LITTLE, BROWN AND COMPANY
IN ASSOCIATION WITH
THE ATLANTIC MONTHLY PRESS

Published simultaneously in Canada
by Little, Brown & Company (Canada) Limited
PRINTED IN THE UNITED STATES OF AMERICA

Once again for
Anne, Paul, and Jane

Contents

HUMBUG
MOUNTAIN

1

The Goose Pull

MY SISTER GLORIETTA came bursting through the front door of Pa's newspaper office. "Wiley!" she cried out. "They've got Mr. Johnson by the neck!"

I was leaning back in Pa's swivel chair with my legs propped up on the southeast corner of Pa's rolltop desk. He'd left me in charge of business affairs and Ma had left me in charge of Glorietta.

I studied her through my bare feet. "Glorietta," I said calmly, and spit in Pa's cuspidor. "Stop your howling. Mr. Johnson's penned up in the backyard with the chickens."

"No, he ain't!" Tears began gully-washing down her cheeks. "He must have got loose! They're fixing to have a goose pull!"

"You know that's not so," I said patiently. Even though I was considerably older than Glorietta — three years and two months — she stood a mite taller than I. It wasn't fair. She was only ten, but skinny-legged and nearsighted. Ma could hardly get her to wear her brass-rimmed spectacles in public; folks called her window-eyes and dumb things like that. The doctor said she'd outgrow the specs, and Pa said I'd shoot up before long. We were both of us infernally impatient.

"A goose pull?" I said. "Glorietta, you know it's not the Fourth of July or anything like that. Mr. Johnson's out back. I watered his tub not an hour ago."

"Maybe you left the gate open!"

I straightened up in the chair. Mr. Johnson was Ma's pet goose. She'd have my hide if anything happened to Mr. Johnson.

"I always latch the gate," I said. "That bull goose is exactly where he ought to be. Come on, I'll show you."

We went out back and the first thing I saw was chickens running loose. The gate had swung open. Mr. Johnson was gone.

This town we lived in, Mulesburg, was an uncommonly backward sort of place. Folks around and about raised mules and turnips and clod-headed mischief. There was hardly a dog that hadn't had a string of tin cans tied to its tail, or a cat either. In Mulesburg a dogfight in the street was considered refined entertainment and drew hat-slapping crowds.

I don't mean to say that Mulesburg was our home. Ma could never get Pa to stay in one place long enough to call it home. Newspapermen are born with the yonders. Pa was that way — itchy-footed, long-strided, and with his dark eyes always drawn to the horizon.

And I'll have to confess that more than once we were run out of town. Newspapering was a risky profession, and Pa carried a short pepperbox pistol handy in his brown corduroy coat. I've seen men come looking for him with a horsewhip or worse just because Pa had said in print they were lop-eared donkeys or corn-cribbing crooks. Newspapermen are given to strong language like that.

"Fellow's got no sense of humor," Pa would say, after he'd scared them off with his six-barreled pepperbox. The little thing shot every which way, which made it almighty hair-raising. "But wasn't he sizzling mad! Hotter'n the devil in long woolen underwear. No point in waiting around for the tar and feathers."

And we'd pack. We had an ol' Washington hand press and three cases of lead type, and Pa could start up another newspaper quicker'n a hen lays an egg.

We got stuck in Mulesburg because Glorietta broke out with the measles. We were only just passing through, heading west, and Pa discovered the town didn't have a newspaper.

Ma put Glorietta to bed and Pa started up the *Mulesburg Squibob*. He fancied names like that.

It didn't take long to discover why the place had no reading matter of its own. The first issue of the *Squibob* was as easy to hand out as a hot horseshoe.

Hardly anyone in Mulesburg could read.

Pa never laughed so hard as when the laugh was on him. "Why, folks in this cussed town consider anyone fully educated who can count to twenty without taking off his shoes!" he had said.

The local people resented the *Squibob* right off. We were outsiders, to begin with, but what put an arch in their backs was that a newspaper in town made them aware of their own howling ignorance. It's true, a few folks took a different view and began sending their children to school

5

more than one day a month. "We've performed a public service," Pa declared airily. "A noble profession, newspapering."

But on the whole we were as popular as a skunk at a lawn party. We'd have been up and gone by now except that someone had burned our wagon to the ground. It didn't surprise me now that someone had made off with Mr. Johnson.

"Hurry!" Glorietta said.

A goose pull. The only thing I could think of to do was fetch my hickory slingshot and fill my back pocket with broken lead type. Then we lit out. It surprised me to see that Glorietta had put on her brass specs without being told.

"They went this way, Wiley!"

There were mud puddles here and there, but on the whole the roads were drying out. It didn't take us long to find Mr. Johnson.

We could hear him honking away something fierce even before we saw him. We hauled up about a quarter of a mile west of town and kept to the trees and bushes. About six men were sitting their fastest mules, waiting for the goose pull to start.

All we could see of Mr. Johnson was his long neck rising out of the center of the road. They had smeared his neck with black grease and had buried the rest of him. The idea was to whip their mules, race for the goose, lean way down and try to catch that weaving, slippery neck. I'm not saying it was easy to do. The first one to snatch the goose out of the ground won the contest. Almost always it broke the goose's neck.

"One at a time, gents, one at a time," Earl-Bob Pickett called out. He appeared to be in charge. "I'll go first."

It was all I could do to keep Glorietta from rushing out there. Earl-Bob Pickett was already whipping his mule and she'd get run down. He was a round, fat-backed little man and came thundering down the road like the devil beating tanbark.

I was already loading my slingshot with broken lead. From the cover of the bushes I drew back. As he leaned over for Mr. Johnson's greased neck I let fly a broadside.

I missed. But he missed too. The other men raised a laugh and a hoot, and another mule came fast-trotting down the road.

"I'd best get closer," I told Glorietta, and we both dodged behind another bush. Mr. Johnson was honking and weaving his neck about like a teased snake.

It was Earl-Bob's younger brother Froy riding that second mule. He came toward us, whooping and hollering, and I followed him with my slingshot. The moment I had a clear target of his back I let go.

He missed Mr. Johnson by a mile. I didn't miss Froy Pickett. He kept up the whooping and hollering, only his voice had risen to a pig squeal, and he slapped at his back. "I'm bee-stung!" he cried out.

The goose-pullers kept coming, one after the other, and by time Earl-Bob's turn came round again I was down to the last bits of broken type in my pocket. Mr. Johnson still hadn't been snatched up, though I'd missed as often as not.

Then I noticed that Earl-Bob began to slow his mule as he approached Mr. Johnson. He meant to have that

goose. I disliked to do it, but I aimed at the rump of his mule.

That mule took off as if he were shot from a stovepipe. It caught Earl-Bob by enormous surprise. I don't know how long he hung on, for that runaway mule disappeared around a bend in the road.

And around the bend up loomed Pa and Ma in an old freight wagon they'd gone to buy.

Glorietta didn't lose a moment. She ran to Mr. Johnson and began digging him loose with her bare hands. And when Ma saw what had been happening she shot those goose-pullers a look hot enough to melt rocks. She was beside Glorietta in no time. "What a pack of howling jackasses!" Ma declared. "And I'm not referring to the mules!"

Pa strode forward, his square-toed boots muddy, his corduroy coat unbuttoned and hanging loose, and the wide knife-blade brim of his hat pulled straight across his eyes. "Howdy, Froy," he said, polite as you please. "Wasn't that your brother Earl-Bob who just went by without tipping his hat?"

"That goose of yours got loose," Froy answered, still clawing at his back. "Nothing meaner than a bull goose. You ought to keep him penned up."

Pa nodded. "Let's apply it all the way around. There's no one meaner than your brother Earl-Bob. And he's loose down the road. Pen him up, Froy, pen him up. For if I catch sight of him I intend to dig a hole and grease his neck. You'll all be invited to the man pull. Good day, gentlemen."

When we got back to town and Ma discovered I'd been shooting lead type at grown men she wanted to take the slingshot away from me. But Pa said, "Wiley did those rascals a favor, Jenny. They'll get their first reading lesson plucking type out of each other's hide."

2

On the Road

THERE WAS a whistle of rain a couple of days later when we left Mulesburg — forever.

The freight wagon Pa had bought was yellow where any paint was left sticking. He greased the hubs while the horses were getting shod. Ma had cleaned Mr. Johnson with homemade glycerine soap and warm water. Finally Glorietta and I rounded up the chickens.

Glorietta's fingers kind of froze at her neck and an awful sick look came over her face. "It's gone, Wiley. I've lost my locket!"

We searched all over for it. The locket was a little lump of gold, no bigger'n a watermelon seed, but almighty precious to her. Grandpa had sent it to her when she was five.

We even went back to the trees and bushes we'd hidden in during the goose pull. But that locket was nowhere. Finally dark was coming on and even Glorietta gave up. I could tell she was trying hard not to flood up any tears. She was going to have to leave her gold locket behind in Mulesburg.

We were up before first light loading the wagon with the printing press, type, a keg of powdered ink, newsprint, Pa's spittoon, Pa's books of Shakespeare and Homer, a stack of door signs, our few sticks of furniture, two crates of chickens, Mr. Johnson, Mr. Johnson's oaken water tub, pots and pans, Ma's piano music, a sack of flour, a sack of cornmeal, a sack of coffee beans, and two horsehair trunks. Ma also found room for her flowerpots.

I helped Pa hitch up our two big iron-gray horses. Ma was wearing her dark traveling dress with what always looked to me like a spiderweb of white lace up around her neck. She pinned her hat through her reddish hair and touched up the dove feathers. Then she pulled down the green shades of the *Mulesburg Squibob* and we were ready to travel.

But Pa didn't consider it right and proper to depart without leaving a message. He thumbed through our own printed signs, chose one to his liking, and hung it on the doorknob.

OUT TO LUNCH

Col. Rufus Flint
Poet, Editor, & Publisher

Ma opened her black umbrella against the first splatters of rain and Pa climbed up beside her on the spring seat. He shook the leather reins and we were off at last. Glorietta and I sat on the tailgate, with our legs dangling over and our heads snugged under the freight canvas. Ten minutes later Mulesburg disappeared from sight behind us.

The first weeds of spring were up. Before long the rain

squall whisked itself away and the sun broke out, warm and fresh. We were heading west again.

I dug around under the canvas for my nickel novels. I was collecting the complete adventures of Quickshot Billy Bodeen. I had only four books. There were heaps more to find. Pa, with his poet's eye, declared them mangy trash, but I read them anyway. I guess Pa was kind of famous, but I'd never met anyone who'd read his poems. When the mood seized him he'd scratch out page after page of his new poem. It was perishing long, and not even half finished.

"Do you want to hear *Quickshot Billy, King of the Tin Stars?*" I asked Glorietta.

She was still in the dismals about leaving her locket behind. "You've read that a dozen times," she said.

"How about *Quickshot Billy and the Robbers of Outlaw Gulch?*"

"Oh, nausea," she groaned.

"They're true stories," I said. "He's a real man."

"Ugh."

Sometimes there was no reasoning with Glorietta. But we had slathers of time to pass so I turned back the paper cover of *Quickshot Billy, Marshal of the Wild Frontier,* and cleared my throat. "Chapter One," I said.

"I'm going to put my fingers in my ears."

"Go ahead," I said, and began to read aloud. " 'Quickshot Billy Bodeen stood straight as a pine, arms akimbo, his iron jaw set, waiting, waiting —' "

"What does *akimbo* mean?"

"How can you hear with fingers in your ears?"

"No real person would ever stand with his arms akimbo," she declared. "I'll bet it's a made-up word."

"It means elbows out."

"Hogwash."

"Ask Pa. Quickshot Billy is about to draw his guns, that's why he's standing arms akimbo."

"And no real person has an iron jaw. That's enough to make a cat laugh. It would rust like an old hinge."

"His jaw is not *made* of iron," I said. "It's just set like iron. Hard. Determined. He wouldn't be smiling at a time like that."

"That's the trouble. Quickshot Billy never smiles. And there are never any girls in those stories."

"It's the wild frontier. That's no place for women."

"There must be at least one," Glorietta insisted. "Maybe two. But they wouldn't have anything to do with a cluck like Quickshot Billy, always standing with his arms akimbo. And he hasn't once taken a bath in any of those fiddle-faddle books. I'll bet he smells like skunk cabbage."

"Sure," I said. "He stops right in the middle of a gun-fight to take a bath. I'm going to read to myself."

"I'd be *ever* so much obliged, Wiley."

I clamped my jaws and went on with the story. The best thing to do was ignore her. At times like that I sorely missed not having someone my own age to talk to. We jumped around so much I was always an outsider. It didn't matter that Quickshot Billy Bodeen was a grown man; I'd come to feel he was my closest friend. My only friend, I guess. I never had to leave him behind, either.

After a while Glorietta got tired of watching our freshly cut wheel tracks in the road. "Wiley?" she muttered.

14

That arch-villain of the border, Hognose Jack, had dodged into one of the dusty cross streets and planned to make a target of Quickshot Billy's back.

"Wiley?" Glorietta said again. "What exactly does *bankrupt* mean?"

I didn't look up. Quickshot Billy wore a finger ring with a little mirror in it, and in a few seconds he'd catch the reflection of Hognose Jack lurking behind him. I turned the page and Quickshot Billy fired his pistol over his shoulder.

"What does *bankrupt* mean, Wiley?"

"Insolvent," I answered. "Be quiet."

Of course, Quickshot Billy only grazed him, with just that ring mirror to aim by. But Hognose Jack lit out of there like a jackrabbit.

"What in tarnation does *insolvent* mean?" Glorietta murmured.

"Bankrupt," I answered. "What are you whispering for?"

"Pa's bankrupt," she said.

I slid her a look. "You don't know what you're talking about. It means when you're flat out of money. Not even enough to buy a stick of candy."

"I woke up in the night and heard them talking. That's what Pa said. Bankrupt."

"You must have heard wrong," I said. Pa always had a jingle of coins in his pocket.

"Why do you suppose they went to the county seat yesterday?"

"To buy this freight wagon."

She shook her head. "They tried to sell those six town lots we own in Sunrise."

"Glorietta, you dreamt it. Ma wouldn't let Pa sell off those lots.

Ma always talked about Sunrise as if it were our own promised land. It was a brand-new city our grandfather, Captain Tuggle, had staked out somewhere along the Missouri River. That was three years ago. We had a big, rolled-up colored lithograph picture of the town showing Grandpa's very own riverboat, the *Phoenix,* tied up at the landing. He'd given us six of the finest lots on a bluff over-looking the hotel and opera house. Someday we'd haul up there and build a great house and Ma could have a piano and plant flowers all over the place. She was always plant-ing gardens, but we were generally up and gone before the flowers were ready to pick. No, Ma would never let loose of our Sunrise property. Those lots were uncommonly im-portant to her.

"I didn't say Pa *sold* them," Glorietta said. "No one around here would buy them. Sunrise is too dreadfully far off."

"Glorietta, you're just making things up to pass the time. Pa paid cash money for this wagon, didn't he? We're not busted."

"I suppose I'm making up that he's not wearing his gold watch and chain this morning."

I could hear a distant clap of thunder, but it was all in-side my head.

"He sold them off for traveling money," Glorietta said.

We stopped in one town after another. We'd let Mr. Johnson swim around in a horse trough while Pa scouted about, looking for Opportunity. He always pronounced the word with a capital *O*.

He'd return with a larksome smile. "Another Mulesburg," he'd say, and we'd move on. Some of those towns had newspapers, and we could all set type — especially Ma. She was wondrously quick at it. Glorietta and I had both learned to read by sorting spilled type. But Pa wouldn't hire us out. He didn't say anything, but I could tell there had been opportunities. But not Opportunity.

I always felt a mite uneasy whenever Pa was out of sight. It was something Glorietta and I hardly ever talked about. Pa had a way of disappearing. Sometimes for weeks at a time. We never knew when he walked out the door if we'd ever see him again. Even in these little towns I felt a huge relief when I caught sight of him returning to the wagon.

We camped out every night. Ma made a kind of merry time of it. She said it didn't bother her a bit when we heard strange noises in the dark. "Why, there's no better watchdog than a goose," she smiled. "And Mr. Johnson's the best."

Day after day we were getting dustier and dirtier. Finally, miles from anywhere and with night coming on, there rose up a narrow, slab-sided building with a tall false front at the edge of the road. It didn't seem to belong there. It looked like a building that had wandered away from town and got lost.

Pa pulled up and we all gazed at the sign. Glorietta peered through her glasses and said, "It's spelled wrong."

THE SURE ENUF HOTEL

Pa beat the dust out of his hat and Ma laughed. "It's spelled right enough for the occasion," she said. "And 'sure enuf,' that's where this family is going to stay the night."

We took baths, and after dinner Pa unrolled the colored lithograph and stared at it. Then he cleared his throat.

"Wiley," he said. "Glorietta. Your mother and I have hit upon a splendid notion. Opportunity? Why, Opportunity's been hiding right under our noses. Sunrise! At the foot of Humbug Mountain. That's where we'll head. To Sunrise — the Parnassus of the West!"

3

The *Prairie Buzzard*

SOON AFTER DAYBUST we left the Sure Enuf Hotel. We were in high good spirits. I don't think even Pa knew *exactly* where Sunrise was, but we were bound to find it once we reached the Missouri River. We'd board a steamboat in St. Louis and buy passage straight to the Parnassus of the West.

"Nausea," Glorietta muttered. She had become uncommonly fond of that word. "What'll Grandpa think when he sees me in these ugly spectacles?"

"They're not ugly."

"*Infernally* ugly. He'll think I'm homelier'n a basket of knotholes."

"Oh, nausea yourself," I said. "That's the dumbest thing I ever heard."

She spread her toes and stared at them. "I wrote him a letter last Christmas. He didn't answer."

"Of course not. Town builders hardly have time to stop for air, let alone scratch out a lot of mail. But there could be a whole tote of letters floating around, trying to catch up with us."

She shrugged. "He'll be mad that I lost my locket he gave me."

"Stop pining about it," I said. "Won't he be surprised

when we turn up! I'll bet he'll give us free rides on his steamboat. We'll go skimming up and down the river like high-lightning. Maybe he'll let me steer."

She looked up from her toes. "What about me?"

"You too," I said.

By the time we reached St. Louis I had charged through all four adventures of Quickshot Billy — again. I wished I had a finger ring with a mirror so I could see behind me. Outlaws were common as crows out west and a thing like that might come in handy. But Pa said he didn't think Captain Tuggle would allow outlaws inside the city limits. Grandpa was strong as a bull, and when he gave an order the blast of his voice set windmills spinning ten miles away.

And he might be right here in St. Louis to pick up a cargo of supplies or something. That would be a great stroke of happenstance! The first thing Pa did was buy a newspaper for Ma. She quickly turned to the shipping list. Glorietta and I hung over her shoulders as she ran her finger down the column of arrivals and departures. The *Phoenix* wasn't there.

"Oh drat," Ma declared. She wasn't usually given to intemperate language of that nature.

Pa put us up in Planters Hotel and took me along the levee to choose a steamboat. We moved at a great clip — Pa was a high-headed sort of man with a brisk stride — and hauled up at a side-wheeler with most of the paint curling off. It looked like it was molting.

"Wiley, how does that vessel take your fancy?" he asked.

It was a pestiferous old boat that wouldn't hold a candle to Grandpa's *Phoenix*. But I said, "Fine, Pa," and we walked aboard.

The captain was sitting in the shade of a tattered awning. He was of monstrous size and was trying to button a little wing collar and not choke himself in the bargain.

Pa pulled the newspaper out of his coat pocket. "I see by the public prints, sir, that you depart upriver tomorrow evening."

"A misprint, sir," the captain said. He seemed a friendly sort. "I depart when I get this confounded collar buttoned. That could take a week."

"Soon enough," Pa grinned. "I'd like to book cabin passage to Sunrise."

The left wing of the collar sprang loose. "Ah, the scoundrels! They've shrunk my collars. Sunrise, did you say? I know every snag and sandbar on the Mississippi, sir, and I've never heard of Sunrise."

"Hardly surprising," Pa said. "It's on the Missouri."

The other wing of his starched collar popped. "The Missouri! Sir, do you take me for a confounded blockhead? That's not a river. It's a shifty, half-bred, half-born, sand-clogged abomination. It chews up riverboats for breakfast and picks its teeth with the jack staffs. Why, I'd no more head this splendid craft into the Missouri than tie up to a tree full of woodpeckers."

"Are you saying, sir, that it's unnavigable?" Pa remarked.

"Only eight months of the year. Then it's so shallow you have to spit over the side to raise the water level." The captain's plump fingers had finally got hold of both ends of his collar. "But you're in luck. It's in spring flood. You'll find a few confounded fools along the levee who enjoy playing hide and seek with those Missouri currents and sandbars."

Grandpa a confounded fool? I spoke up, brushing the lank hair out of my eyes. "Maybe you haven't had the pleasure of meeting Captain Tuggle, sir. He's my grandpa and he's almighty *fond* of the Missouri River. Prefers it, in fact. I reckon he considers the Mississippi too tame to fool with."

Pa gave me a one-eyed look. I suppose I was laying it on too thick. The captain got his collar buttoned at last and broke into a smile. "Your own grandsir, is he? Didn't mean to offend you, lad. I remember Captain Tuggle well enough. Reputation finer'n silk. None better. Why, your grandsir could steer a boat over nothing deeper than a heavy dew with room to spare. Haven't seen him about in years. Gone up the Big Muddy, has he? To Sunrise?"

"The Parnassus of the West," I nodded. "And that's where we aim to go."

"Hunt up the *Amos Pikes* or the *Marigold*. They've been running the Missouri. There's also the *Prairie Buzzard,* but I don't recommend it. The captain cheats at cards."

The *Amos Pikes* was undergoing repairs. It had just come down the Missouri from way up in Montana Territory and the captain said he wouldn't go back up if they hung candy on trees. The master of the *Marigold* had never heard of Sunrise, nor Humbug Mountain neither. He couldn't find them on his charts, but that didn't surprise me. The charts of the river were so fly-squashed and food-splattered I don't think he could find St. Louis if he weren't already moored there. Anyway, he said he wouldn't venture farther west than Kansas City. That left us the *Prairie Buzzard*.

It was a dirty, trampish stern-wheeler with chalky white animal bones heaped on deck. Piles of them — skulls and all. Roustabouts were heaving the bones into freight wagons alongside.

I can't say I liked the sight of that boat, or the captain either. He was a short, long-nosed man with oyster-pale eyes and a sweaty bald head. But he did favor us with a smile when we stepped aboard. At least, I think it was a smile.

"Captain Cully, at your service," he said in a voice soft as goose grease.

"Colonel Rufus Flint, sir," Pa said. "Will you be departing for the Upper Missouri in the near future, Captain Cully?"

"As soon as these buffalo bones get unloaded."

"You deal in a surprising cargo, sir."

"What's surprising about buffalo bones? Off they goes to the fertilizer factory. Prairie gold to my way of thinking, Colonel, prairie gold. I buy and sell — and take a passenger or two when the price is right, if that's what's on your mind."

"It is, sir," Pa said. "Sunrise is our destination. It doesn't seem to be on the river charts."

"I don't use charts," Captain Cully scoffed. "Charts'll wreck your boat. The Big Muddy ain't *never* held still long enough to have its picture drawn, Colonel. But I recollect Sunrise and I'll guarantee to set you down at the landing — if the price is right."

"And what would the right price be?" Pa asked.

I think Captain Cully had already calculated what he might squeeze out of Pa, for the figure was waiting at the tip of his tongue. "One hundred and fifty dollars a head, Colonel, and eighty cents a hundredweight for your freight and baggage."

"Most reasonable, sir," Pa remarked, to my astonishment. And to Captain Cully's, too. "A decided bargain. Will there be other passengers aboard?"

"I pick up and drop off a chap now and then."

Pa looked crestfallen. "Only a few? Well, that is a disappointment. A river trip is most tiresome without fellow passengers to take a hand at cards. Cards, sir, are my joy and my folly. I've lost six or eight tidy fortunes at the gaming table. I'm sorry, Captain, but I must decline your generous offer."

Captain Cully's pale little eyes began to flutter with confusion. He wasn't going to let a man who had lost six or eight fortunes at cards get away. "Hold on, Colonel. I don't mind admitting that I enjoy a game of cards myself — though I'm not very good at it, you understand. Still, we could pass some pleasant hours together."

"I'm afraid not," Pa said. "Your days would be busy with currents and snags and sandbars."

"You come aboard, and I'll shave the price. Why, this is just a fertilizer boat and I oughten to ask first-class fares.

Say thirty-five dollars a head and your freight and baggage free. I'd consider it most gracious if you'd join me upriver, sir, and maybe learn me the fine points of the game."

Pa hesitated so long that Captain Cully's freckled hands got fidgety, and I noticed them for the first time.

"Agreed, sir," Pa said finally. "But only because I'm in some haste to reach Sunrise."

"The *Prairie Buzzard* will be ready to cast off the day after tomorrow."

"Splendid."

But I was hardly listening. The moment I had Pa alone along the levee I said, "Did you see what he had on his finger!"

"A ring."

"Pa, he must have got it from Quickshot Billy himself. *That ring had a mirror in it.*"

That stopped Pa short and he looked at me with a smile lurking in his dark eyes. "Are you dead certain, Wiley?"

"Dead positive."

Pa looked back and then busted into a laugh. "I declare! A shiner! Why, the unspeakable rascal. Thank you, Wiley. That will make it ever so much easier to teach Captain Cully the fine points of the game."

4

The Shiner

WE LEFT ST. LOUIS on a windy spring morning.

As soon as our plunder was loaded aboard, Pa sold off the horses and freight wagon, paid the hotel bill, counted out our steamboat fare into Captain Cully's hands and still had cash left over.

"We won't be needing a freight wagon in Sunrise," Pa said. But I do think he was sorry to give up those matched iron-gray horses.

"Pa, what exactly *is* a shiner?"

He chuckled and gave me a wink. "Be patient. You'll see."

There was no end to things Pa knew about, but he could be infernally shut-mouthed when it pleased him.

"But he cheats, Pa," I said. "You're not going to play cards with Captain Cully?"

"Cheating will make the game ever so much more interesting," he said, and lit a cigar.

I don't think Ma knew about the bargain he'd struck with Captain Cully, for she seemed without a care in the world now that we were on our way to Sunrise. I decided not to open my mouth to Glorietta. They had both bought new hats in St. Louis, and parasols in the bargain, and sat on deck as if we were traveling aboard a grand packet instead of a buffalo-bone boat.

Before long the wharves and warehouses of St. Louis slipped behind us. The *Prairie Buzzard* went snorting up the Mississippi, her stern wheel churning up a muddy bobtail of river water.

I reckon we had steamed five miles or so when Captain Cully stuck his head out of the wheelhouse window and blew the whistle and rang a bell and made as much noise as possible. The black woodsmoke, tumbling upward from the single tin funnel, was shot through with live sparks like fireflies.

We were entering the mouth of the Missouri River.

I found Glorietta beside me, watching the sights through her specs. "Wiley?"

"What?"

"I don't want to go to Sunrise."

I gave her a look. "Grandpa won't think you're ugly. I told you."

"It's not that."

"Doggone it, Glorietta, what's eating you now?"

"What do you think Pa'll do?"

"In Sunrise? Start a newspaper, of course."

"He might leave us, Wiley. The way he has before."

"He didn't walk off and leave us in St. Louis, did he?"

"But there'll be Grandpa to look after us. Pa might *never* come back next time."

I fell silent a long time. Then I shrugged. "Pa cares about us. You know that as well as I do."

Her voice rose a little in the wind. "Then why does he run off?"

"I don't know," I said.

"Do you ever hate him?"

"Doggone it, Glorietta, Pa won't leave us in Sunrise."
I said it as if I really believed it. I was trying hard to.
Maybe Humbug Mountain was exactly the yonder sort of
place in the back of his mind when he'd toss his gaze at
the horizon. There'd be a house to build on one of our
very own lots, the newspaper, plays going on in the opera
house and all manner of things. "You can count on it.
Pa'll stick closer'n paint."

I don't know how far upriver we ventured before night
came on and Captain Cully tied up to a cottonwood
thicket. The Missouri wasn't as fearsome as I had expected. As far as I could tell it was just another river,
though the paddle wheel churned up as much mud as
water. And I reckon the current was uncommonly strong,
for the *Prairie Buzzard* kept yanking at her mooring lines.

We were served a tolerable supper of catfish and common trimmings. I kept looking from Pa to Captain Cully.
They both seemed in high spirits, waiting for the duel
at cards to begin.

I must confess that some folks looked upon Pa as a
thundering-great sinner and pitied Ma. I reckon he gam-
bled at cards and drank whiskey and cussed something
fierce — though not within earshot of women, children, or
dogs.

But I'm certain he never *cheated* at cards, and that's
what worried me. He'd be no match for Captain Cully.
As for those other sins, well — I never saw Pa step out of a

saloon tangle-footed. And all newspapermen cuss, so that can't rightly be held against him.

Suddenly Captain Cully fixed his pale eyes on Glorietta, who hadn't uttered a word throughout the meal. I reckon he meant to be sociable, but Glorietta could be awfully clever about people. It was as if with her weak eyesight she could see clear through strangers. I don't think she liked the sound of his voice, which seemed to come whistling out of his long, thin nose.

"Little lady," he said, and I'm sure it set her teeth on edge. "Little lady, you can pick up heaps of spending money out there on the prairie. I'm referring to buffalo bones. You just stack 'em up like cordwood and when I return downriver I'll pay you four dollars a ton. You'll find them easy, scattered all about."

Glorietta gazed up from her plate. "Why?" she asked.

"Why what, little lady?"

"Why'll we find 'em easy, scattered all about?"

"Because that's the way the buffalo hunters left them," Captain Cully grinned. "Millions of the beasts left to rot, and good riddance."

"But why?" Glorietta said.

"Why? For the buffalo robes! I can tell you there's hardly a buffalo left wearing his own hide. There's just the bones, and I pay four dollars a ton."

"I never heard anything so *dreadful* in my life," Glorietta said flatly. And then she couldn't help laying it on extra thick. "Sir, the buffalo is my *favorite* animal."

She'd never seen a buffalo in her life, but that didn't matter. It was her favorite animal now.

"You'll change your mind, little lady," Captain Cully snickered. "Just stack 'em up like cordwood along the riverbank."

Glorietta kept her nose high in the air. "I'd rather perish than collect buffalo bones, sir."

Of course, Ma put a stop to this brand of table talk, but I must admit I began to favor Glorietta's side of the argument. In Quickshot Billy's stories buffaloes blackened the hills for miles on end. I was disappointed to learn there was nothing left but bones lying about in the sun.

Finally Ma and Glorietta retired to our cabin and Pa lit a thin cigar. The table was cleared and Captain Cully lost no time in slapping a greasy pack of cards on the table.

"What's your game, Colonel?"

"Poker, as a rule, Captain," Pa said. "But it wouldn't be fair. You were honest enough to confess that you are not adept with the pasteboards."

"Pasteboards?"

"Cards. The devil's fifty-two. Perhaps we had best engage in a harmless sport. Dominoes, perhaps?"

"That's mighty considerate of you, Colonel. But no, poker will do. I'm anxious for anything you can learn me."

I could hardly take my eyes off Captain Cully. He was acting infernally innocent, but clearly gloating to himself. He'd skin Pa with his cheating tricks.

"Well, if it's a lesson in cards you want," Pa said, with the cigar lightly clamped between his teeth, "I'm glad to be of service. We'll play with pennies."

Captain Cully scratched his bald head. "Pennies? Why, gracious me, Colonel, cartwheels and gold pieces will suit me. I don't mind paying proper for my education."

31

"As you wish," Pa said. They both dug cash money out of their pockets and made little stacks on the table.

Captain Cully shuffled the mangy deck, handed it to Pa for the cut, and began dealing. But he had hardly started when Pa stopped him. "Captain, you've already made your first mistake."

Captain Cully looked up as if he'd been caught with his hand in someone's pocket. "Me, sir?"

"You, sir. Decidedly."

"I declare. Shall I start over?"

Pa shifted the cigar to the other side of his mouth. He was smiling ever so slightly. "I'm referring to your present opponent, Captain. Your obedient servant. Me, sir. You didn't look at my hands."

"Your hands?"

"I don't have to tell you that rogues and scoundrels abound at the gaming table. Take my advice, Captain. Always look at a man's hands. He might be wearing a shiner. A mirror ring."

The silence was so sudden and Captain Cully sat so still you'd think he was posing for a photographer and trying not to blink. For the first time I saw that Pa was wearing a ring. A brand-new silver one.

"A shiner?" Captain Cully said. His voice was so weak he couldn't have blown out a match if he'd swallowed it.

Pa turned up his left palm and there was the mirror, small and round and bright as a diamond. "Of course, only a crude oaf would resort to such a simpleminded cheat," Pa said. He picked up the pack and began to deal off cards. "But such devices are for sale in St. Louis to would-be cardsharps lacking finer skills. I was sure it would amuse and instruct you, Captain. Notice that I am able to read the reflection of each card as I deal it off to my unwary opponent. That's a shiner, sir — and I believe it's quite legal to shoot a man foolish enough to wear one at the gaming table."

By this time Captain Cully had swallowed his Adam's apple two or three times. You could see the color draining out of his face. His freckled hands were out of sight, under the table, and I believe he was having trouble getting the mirror ring off his own finger.

"Now then," Pa said pleasantly. He tossed me the St. Louis shiner he had bought for the occasion. "Now then, Captain, there are cartwheels and gold pieces waiting on the table to change ownership. I'm looking forward to an enjoyable voyage. Cut the cards."

I never saw such a sudden change come over a man. Captain Cully scooped his money into his hat and jumped up. "Some other time," he scowled. "Feel that blasted river current! We'll be lucky if we don't tear the mooring trees out by the roots. I've boat work to attend to."

He loped away in a burnt hurry. After a moment Pa threw back his head and laughed. "I think we cured him of cardsharping on this trip, Wiley. River current! He went for a hacksaw to get that cheap gambler's ring off."

"Reckon he did," I smiled. I looked longingly at the St. Louis shiner in my hand. I polished the mirror on my sleeve and handed it back.

Pa lit a fresh match to his cigar. "I've no further use for it, Wiley. If you want it, it's yours."

5

Smile, You're in Sunrise

PA WAS RIGHT. The shiner ring disappeared from Captain Cully's finger, and he always seemed to have boat work to do when Pa proposed a game of cards.

I couldn't wait to show my St. Louis shiner to Glorietta.

"Just like Quickshot Billy's," I said.

"What's it for? To look at yourself? I'll bet Quickshot Billy was *always* looking at himself."

"Oh, you're considerable smart," I said. I breathed on the mirror and polished it. "How do you suppose he could shoot back over his shoulder? That's what a shiner's for."

I didn't tell her it was a gambler's ring. I was certain a famous lawman like Quickshot Billy would never cheat at cards.

Of course, the ring was miles too big for me, but I got some of Ma's embroidery thread and wrapped it around and around the band for a good snug fit. All the way up the Missouri I practiced seeing behind me. I saw lots of ducks and geese and even some white pelicans that way.

We were almost a week reaching Kansas City. Captain Cully didn't stop there even to take on cordwood. He steamed on by the woodyards and kept going as if the law were waiting for him. And I reckon it should have been.

He never once bought wood for the furnace. He just helped himself to anything unguarded along the banks that would burn. There were deserted homesteaders' cabins and half-sunk old riverboats that had run afoul of snags and whatnot. He'd send out his wrecking crew and before long everything but the windows went up through the *Prairie Buzzard*'s black smokestack.

He went zigzagging up the Missouri, dodging floating logs and things I couldn't see at all — shoals, I guess. He'd laugh when we passed another boat hung up on a fresh sandbar, as if it would be a wood feast for his wreckers on the return trip. He steered his own boat cleverly, following the shifting channel like a dog following a scent. I'll have to give him his due. He seemed able to outthink that river.

Every night the boiler had to be cleaned out, for it kept filling with Missouri mud. We charged past Nebraska City and Council Bluffs and kept going. After that the river towns seemed to get smaller and farther apart, as if we were running out of civilization.

In the evenings, before darkness fell, Pa usually read Shakespeare to us, or Homer. It wasn't always clear to me what was going on in those stories. But Pa had a real actor's voice, and it was fun to listen to him.

Glorietta and I spent a good deal of time poring over the colored lithograph of Sunrise, with all its street names, a green park — and Humbug Mountain, with a dazzling cap of snow.

"That's the funniest name for a mountain," Glorietta said.

It was peculiar-sounding, but I said, "If you had a mountain to name what would *you* call it — 'Morning Glory' or 'Buttercup' or something sickening like that?"

Ma glanced up from the book she was reading. It was one of Pa's books of poems. She read them over and over the way I did my nickel novels. "Children, there may be inaccuracies on that lithograph. Town promoters are inclined to brag."

"But Grandpa wouldn't lie," Glorietta said.

"No," Ma answered. "But the artist may have fancied things up a bit. I'll be surprised to find Sunrise quite so grand. Let's wait and see."

We had to do an infernal amount of waiting. Day after day we went winding up the river, thumping and splashing around snags and bobbing tree roots. Sioux City came and went and finally I asked Captain Cully, "Sir, is it much farther to Sunrise?"

He looked down his long, thin nose at me and grinned in an overly friendly way. "Why, we ain't even to the Vermillion River yet."

And after the mouth of the Vermillion slipped behind us he gave me that same grin. "Sunrise? Why, we ain't even in Yankton yet."

But Sunrise didn't turn up after Yankton. Captain Cully seemed to do an awful lot of grinning now. He had some trick up his sleeve, I thought.

The countryside had flattened out all around us. I couldn't spy a hill, let alone a mountain. Captain Cully stayed up in the pilothouse mostly, spitting tobacco juice out the windows, and you had to be careful how you approached.

"Sir," I said at last. "Are you certain we didn't pass Sunrise far back?"

His grin gave way to a chuckle. "Son," he answered, "this river must be twenty-five hundred miles long — and I know every *foot* of it. Sunrise? There's a big ol' mulberry tree I've tied up to many a time. I'll be putting you ashore in no time."

A heavy mist lay over the river the next morning. The *Prairie Buzzard* crept along slower'n a snail. At the bow one of the deckhands kept poking a stick in the water and we felt our way around the bends like a blind man tapping a cane.

Finally there came a jingle of bells and the dark, ghostly shape of a great tree rose up on the left bank. Lines were quickly wrapped around the trunk, and then Captain Cully spit out the window.

"Sunrise, folks!" he called.

"Possibly," Pa answered. In that river fog Captain Cully might be pleased to let us off in the middle of nowhere.

"Take a lantern and see for yourself, Colonel."

I followed Pa ashore and there, nailed to the mulberry tree, hung a sign.

Smile, You're in Sunrise

As soon as our belongings were set ashore the mooring lines were loosened and the *Prairie Buzzard* crawled away through the mist. But not before Captain Cully tipped his cap and shouted, "Four dollars a ton for buffalo bones — be glad to do business with you!"

Once the riverboat disappeared we made a discovery. There was no regular landing — just the sturdy old mulberry for boats to tie up to. And wherever Sunrise was, it wasn't on the riverbank the way the picture showed.

As we began to explore around for the town, Glorietta slipped off her brass-rimmed spectacles. She wasn't going to meet Grandpa with window-eyes. The fog spread only a short distance beyond the riverbank and we walked smack into fresh morning sunlight.

Pa took a slow look around. We all looked around. The only thing to be seen across the flat prairie was a string of cottonwoods to the south a mile or so off. Maybe that's where we'd find Sunrise.

But when we approached all we found were old wooden surveyor's stakes in the ground marking off the grassy city lots. There was no opera house. There were no fine homes. There were no streets.

There was no town. Sunrise was just a scrap of paper.

"There's not even a mountain," I said, and Glorietta slipped her glasses back on to look for herself.

Pa shoved back his hat and laughed. "I expect that's why they named it Humbug Mountain!"

We'd startled a few jackrabbits and a couple of bobtailed deer. We could hear the soft, sad call of mourning doves hidden in the spring grass. And that's all there was in Sunrise. Except us. Grandpa may have had the lots staked out, but he was gone now.

You'd think Ma would have busted into tears, but she

didn't. I know for certain she'd been dreaming of this day for all of three years. And now it had arrived.

She glanced at the weed-grown lots and lifted her chin. "Well, as long as we're in Sunrise — we might as well smile," she said.

6

Fate of the *Phoenix*

THE NEXT THING I knew, Ma had turned her head and was crying softly. Pa took a clutch on her shoulder and they walked off a little way. Glorietta looked at me and I looked at Glorietta. We had never seen her cry before. Not even those times when Pa disappeared.

I turned my back, stuck my fists in my pockets, and took off for the cottonwoods. It was a moment before I realized that Glorietta was following along behind me. We were both clean-scrubbed and fussed up in our Sunday clothes, and that seemed to make everything worse.

"Go ahead and bawl if you want to," I said.

"Didn't know I had to get your permission," she answered. "Where you going?"

"Nowhere."

"I'll go too."

I tossed the hair out of my eyes. Where there was a meander of trees there must be a creek, I thought, and I'd skip a few stones.

I set a good pace, but Glorietta kept up on her spindly legs. "What do you reckon we'll do now?" she murmured.

"Can't stay here, can we?"

"No."

"Then don't ask dumb questions."

41

She fell silent. For about three seconds. "It might be a pesky long wait for another riverboat."

"Might be."

We went crackling through a tangle of willows and cottonwoods, and came to the high bank of the creek. I stopped short and so did Glorietta. The creek was vastly broad and vastly disappointing.

"It's dried up," she said.

"I can see that for myself."

The bottom mud had shrunk and cracked and was curled like dead, brown leaves. But we sat on the bluff and chunked a few stones anyway.

Suddenly a voice shot through the still air.

"Shagnasty!"

I jumped up like a cat out of a woodbox and so did Glorietta. Then the voice came again, but from a fresh quarter.

"Fool Killer! Hang'm! Bash'm!"

It was a croaking, graveyard kind of voice — daft and scaresome. My eyes flicked from tree to tree, but I couldn't catch sight of anyone. Then it came again.

"Shagnasty! Fool Killer!"

We scrambled down the bank and peered back. I didn't believe in haunts, but there was something mighty peculiar roving about in those trees.

Glorietta gave me a look and a whisper. "Oughten we to run for it, Wiley?"

"Unless it's Grandpa," I said.

"Grandpa?"

"Talking to himself. Out of his wits or something."

Then there came a sudden rustle of leaves. Glorietta lit

out across the creek bed and I might have been right beside her — but I saw it.

A crow. Nothing but a big ol' crow.

It rose through the treetops into the sunlight. A he-crow, I thought — it must have had a wingspread of about three feet. Then four or five other crows came flapping after it.

"Hang'm!"

"Bash'm!"

"Caw-caw-caw!"

I stood up and spit angrily. I didn't enjoy being scared out of my wits by a flock of common crows, but it was surprising to meet up with birds that spoke the English language.

"Hey, Glorietta!" I yelled. "Come on back! It's nothing! Only a bunch of infernal crow birds!"

She was almost out of sight around a bend in the creek. But she stopped without looking back at me. Something farther along had caught her eye. She stood fixed where she stood.

"Wiley!" she yelled. "Look! Look what I found!"

The morning sun flashed off her glasses, and then she disappeared around the bend.

So I ran along the creek bed too. And the birds followed along, caw-cawing.

It wasn't a moment before I cut around the bend and hauled up short.

Before me, not fifty yards off, stood a riverboat.

It stood sunk and dry on the creek bottom. Mooring lines swung like strands of a great spiderweb from the trees along the bank. Weeds and creepers had grown up through the huge side wheels. I looked at the empty pilothouse windows, streaked with dirt. I'd never seen such a lonely and forlorn boat. You could tell it had once been pluckish and grand; it was fancied up with lacy-cut woodwork. But now the white paint hung in peels and tatters like a snake shedding its skin.

Glorietta was out of breath when we joined up and stepped closer. The crows fluttered down, taking perches like vultures on the crown of the smokestack.

I gave a shout. "Hello, the boat!"

Silence. We moved nearer and I called again.

"No one there," Glorietta said.

"Must be. Someone taught those crows to speak." I tried again, cupping my hands. "Anybody here?"

"Fool Killer!" The big he-crow was at it again.

We made tracks along the flat hull and looked up at the wooden nameplate hanging on the side of the pilothouse. The weathered gold letters gave me a start, and Glorietta too.

It was the *Phoenix*.

Grandpa's boat.

7

The Fool Killer

GLORIETTA RAN BACK to fetch Pa and Ma. A splintery old gangplank stretched between the creek bluff and the middle deck, and I walked aboard.

"Grandpa?" I called out. "Grandpa, it's me — Wiley."

The deck was gritty under my feet. Windblown dirt covered everything and was piled up like sand dunes against the cabins. I saw footprints. Lots of them, going and coming and scuffled about in the dust. They struck me as almighty fresh.

"Grandpa!"

I had no more than got the word out of my mouth when a hand snatched me by the collar, jerked me off my feet, and held me aloft like a kicking rabbit.

"Cuss'd little varmint!" came a dry whisper at my ear. "What for you sneaking around here?"

He twisted me around to take a closer look. I gazed back at a pair of mean, deep-sunk little eyes and a mouthful of yellow teeth. He was tall and dreadfully skinny — as if he had the dry wilts. Stringy red hair shot down from under the brim of his floppy hat. He had a long horse-face and long bare feet. He was dressed in rags.

My heart was banging so loud he must have been able

45

to hear it. I swallowed hard and managed to say, "This is my grandpa's boat."

"Ain't no grandpas around here."

"Then reckon I better be going. If you'll kindly put me down."

Those deep eyes of his didn't blink any more'n a lizard's.

"Who are you?" I muttered.

It was an eternity before he answered. Finally, in that whispery voice of his, he said, "The Fool Killer."

I think I stopped breathing. As far back as I could remember I'd heard tales of the Fool Killer. He was supposed to carry a bur-oak club on his shoulder and wander the countryside searching for fools. He'd smite them on the head. He was always barefoot, and he had such a long jaw he could eat oats out of a nose bag. Pa said there was no such real creature as the Fool Killer, but the hair on my neck had gone as stiff as hog bristles. This barefoot man was so long-faced he could eat out of a churn.

He upended me, caught my ankles in his big, rattle-boned hands, and carried me like a dead chicken up some stairs to the top deck. I figured he must be going for his bur-oak club. If I didn't do something quick I was done for.

From one smokestack the crows began to squawk again.

"Fool Killer!"

"Bash'm!"

His hands were powerful as iron chain. I was in a blue fright. If only I'd thought to glance at my mirror ring I'd have seen him come ghosting up behind me.

He'd have to let go of my ankles when he fetched up his

club, I thought. And I'd be off quicker'n high-lightning.

The Fool Killer kicked open a door. From inside came a thunderous snort and snoring.

"Shagnasty," the Fool Killer called out.

We were in the pilothouse. I could make out the tall oaken steering wheel, and daylight aglow at the huge windows. Then I saw a man rouse himself from a bedroll on the floor.

"Cuss it all, Fool Killer," he said. "Can't a gentleman take a wink of sleep around here?"

"I catched me another fool," said the Fool Killer.

"Don't look like nothing but a shirttail boy. Set him down."

The Fool Killer kicked the door shut and swung me rightside up. For the first time I got a square look at Mr. Shagnasty. He wore a mangy old bearskin coat and he was big around as a sauerkraut barrel. His beard was dirt-brown and greasy and all a'tangle, like the hairs on a smelly old billy goat.

"Fool Killer," he snorted. "Ain't you got more sense than to bring him aboard? You give away our hideout."

"I spied him cat-footing around."

The other man fixed his eyes on me and hitched up his gunbelt. "Is that a fact?"

"No sir," I said. "I wasn't sneaking about. I was walking plain as day. But I reckon my grandpa's nowhere around, so I'll just be going."

"Well, now, sonny, it's a mite late for that." Mr. Shagnasty pulled out a blue bandanna and gave his lumpy nose a thunderous honk. He wasn't wearing a shirt; just long red underwear, and it was so full of holes you'd think he carried his own moths. "You know who we are," he said.

I answered quickly. "No sir, I don't."

" 'Course you do! Ain't a sheriff anywhere in the territories not looking for the heads of Shagnasty John and the Fool Killer. The terror of the prairies — that's us!"

"I declare," I muttered, struck with awe. I'd never talked to real outlaws before and I was getting all-over lathers of sweat. They were genuine blood-and-thunder badmen. "I won't tell a perishing soul," I added earnestly.

"Can't no boy keep a secret," said the Fool Killer darkly. "Worse'n them crows."

"Nothing we can do about the crows but chunk stones at 'em," Shagnasty John said, scratching through his beard. "But dash it all, boy, me and the Fool Killer can't chance you. It don't leave us much choice. You can see that, can't you?"

"No sir," I answered, trying to stretch out the time. "You must be terrible bad shots if you can't shoot those crows."

Shagnasty John rumbled out a laugh. "Oh, we can fire straight enough. Stop edging toward that door! The Fool Killer is kind of gone-minded, sonny, and you don't want him to crack you in two like a chicken bone."

The Fool Killer reached out his long arm and yanked me back. "I'll drop him in the woods with a mighty bash of my club."

"Fool Killer, don't get anxious," said Shagnasty John, regarding me with slow, crafty eyes. The whites were

48

brown-streaked like tobacco stains. "Who you traveling with?"

I'd forgot all about Glorietta gone to fetch Ma and Pa. "I'm purely alone!" I declared.

Shagnasty John snorted. "You don't tell me."

"Yes sir! I run away from home."

"Wearing shoes? And dressed for church? Sonny, you must figure I got no more brains than God gave geese. Fool Killer, see who else is scuttling about."

The Fool Killer let loose of me to peer out the wheel-house windows. I leaped for the door, opened it, banged it shut behind me, and ran like a scared rabbit.

Shagnasty John and the Fool Killer ran thrashing through the cottonwoods after me. But I wasn't in the trees. I'd ducked under a boxed paddle wheel and snugged myself out of sight. But I couldn't stay there. I had to warn Pa.

My heart was banging away something fearful. I hardly waited to catch my breath before I slipped out of hiding, climbed the dry creek bank, and ducked into the trees. I could tell that Shagnasty John and the Fool Killer were some ways off. The crows were flapping over the treetops, following them.

I ran smack into a rope corral. It held two horses. *Their* horses, I thought.

I picked out the spotted mare, grabbed her mane, and heaved myself onto her back. Then I shot out of there lickety-quick.

And along came Pa and Ma and Glorietta! They were

walking through the spring weeds, clear as bull's-eye targets, and not suspecting a thing.

"Go back!" I yelled. "Run!"

But they couldn't fathom what I was yelling about. Or what I was doing on horseback.

Finally I pulled up and slipped off the mare's back. I could hardly believe I'd got this far without Shagnasty John drawing his gun and filling the air with lead.

I danced the horse around broadside to the trees so that we could shelter ourselves behind her.

"There are terrible outlaws back there!" I burst out. "They mean to kill us!"

Ma gave me a startled look. "Now really, Wiley. You must be imagining it."

"I suppose I'm imagining this horse!"

Pa gave the cottonwoods a tight-eyed gaze. "How do you know they're outlaws?"

"They told me, Pa. Shagnasty John and the Fool Killer. Every sheriff in the territories is looking for them. They're using the *Phoenix* for a hideout."

Ma's fingers had crept to her spidery lace collar. "Is Grandpa there?"

"No, Ma."

"There's no such man as the Fool Killer," Pa said.

"There is now, Pa. Peevish and meaner'n a hornet. Both of 'em."

"Wearing guns?"

"Shagnasty John is. The terror of the prairies, he said."

"Never heard of him." Pa stood calm as an owl at midnight. "It baffles me that he didn't pop some lead your way, Wiley. Especially since you rode off on one of their horses."

"He could have been afraid of shooting the mare," Ma said.

"Must have," I said. And yet, I thought, he'd had a clear shot when I'd busted out of the pilothouse — and maybe again before I'd reached the stairway.

"Downright peculiar," Pa remarked, more to himself than us.

"They're over in those trees," I said, pointing. "Where you see the crows. Watching us for sure. Hadn't we better edge back in a hurry?"

"Wiley, there's no place for us to run where they can't find us out here," Pa answered. "It seems to me they'd already be in full view and shooting up a hailstorm — if they could. It's unnatural. Unless their cartridge belts are empty. Did you notice?"

"No, sir."

But the Fool Killer would have armed himself with his bur-oak club, I thought. I glanced at Glorietta. I could see she was feeling scared about the Fool Killer and all the stories we'd heard.

Pa checked his pepperbox pistol. I peered under the horse's belly and spotted the crows. Shagnasty John and the Fool Killer were keeping themselves mouse-quiet.

"We've come this far and we're not turning back," Pa declared. "Not until we find out what happened to your grandfather. He might have left papers aboard. A logbook, certainly. I have an idea I can send those rascals packing." He handed Ma the short, six-barreled pistol. "Don't fire this bric-a-brac unless you've got no choice."

"Rufus," Ma exclaimed. "You're not going out there!"

"I promise you the terrors of the plains are going to be mighty glad to meet me." Pa gave us a wink. "I want all of you to stay put until I settle matters. Shouldn't take five minutes."

And he was gone. He went striding across the bare city limits of Sunrise, the knife-blade brim of his hat cocked at an angle.

8

The Ghost

I WATCHED Pa's lanky, high-headed figure and hoped I'd grow up to be as fearless as that. You'd think he was just going out for a stroll. Before long he disappeared into the cottonwoods.

We waited. I listened for the sudden crack of gunfire. Pa might have miscalculated Shagnasty John and the Fool Killer. A minute passed without a sound reaching us. There was just the crows flapping from one treetop to another.

"Well, don't worry about your Pa," said Ma. "There's more than one way to skin a cat, and he knows them all."

Glorietta couldn't hold back a whisper. "What did the Fool Killer look like?"

"Never mind," I said.

"Was he carrying a bur-oak club?"

"Glorietta, you know he's pure hogwash. Pa said so, didn't he?"

"But you *saw* him, Wiley. Did he have a horse-face? Could he eat out of a nose bag?"

"Be quiet."

For a long while none of us said another word. I was certain a good five minutes had passed. Maybe more. We just watched the trees, getting more and more fidgety.

I turned to Ma. "I could gallop in with the pepperbox pistol."

"Don't talk rubbish."

"That fool killer man is gone-minded. He might be trying to bash Pa over the head. He's infernally bloodthirsty."

Ma was getting edgy. "Pa told us to stay put!"

We waited some more. I never knew time to run so perishing slow. At least there was no crack of gunfire. Pa must have reckoned right that their ammunition was used up. Suddenly I remembered that they had tried to rid themselves of the crows by chunking rocks at them. If Shagnasty John had bullets for his gun, wouldn't he have shot them?

And then we saw Pa.

He came out of the trees on horseback. He was riding as straight-backed as a general of the army. And stepping along behind him came the terrors of the plains like prisoners of war. They were balancing lumber and boat poles on their shoulders.

Pa reined up beside us. He turned to the outlaws. "I want you to meet my family. My wife Jenny, our daughter Glorietta — and you've already met Wiley."

Shagnasty John tipped his ragged old hat. "Howdy, m'am. Pleased to meet you, Miss Glorietta. How-do, Wiley."

I was struck wordless. Pa had tamed them gentle as sheep. It was an eyebrow-lifter.

"Jenny," Pa said, "you three make yourselves at home on the boat. These two neighborly squatters have kindly agreed to move our belongings aboard."

"Anything you say, Colonel," remarked Shagnasty John. "Glad to oblige. Yes indeed, sir, the sooner you get the law off our trail the better." Then he turned to Ma. "The Colonel says you brought along chickens on the hoof. I declare if they don't make the mouth water. Me and Mr. Fool Killer here, we ain't had lead to shoot any wild game in weeks."

The Fool Killer caught hold of the spotted mare. Glorietta was owl-eyed behind her glasses. She stared at him as if he were the devil with his clothes still smoldering from down below.

"Come along," Pa said, and the three men headed toward the river. We stood where we were like fence posts. How Pa had got the best of those outlaws was a wonder. It fogged the brain.

Then Ma gave her head a toss. "I don't know what your Pa is up to, but I do hope he keeps those two men downwind of us. They smell stronger than skunk cabbage. Now then, what's Grandpa's boat doing over in those trees?"

Ma's green eyes wandered sadly from one end of the boat to the other. "The poor old *Phoenix*. She was pretty as a duck on the water. But look at her now. Dirty as a pigsty. Grandpa wouldn't allow it. Something dreadful must have happened. He'd never abandon the *Phoenix*."

He might be dead, I thought. Maybe we all thought it, but no one ventured to say it.

We trooped across the gangplank to the cabin deck. "Pa said the logbook might tell us a thing or two," I muttered.

Ma nodded. "In Grandpa's stateroom. Or up in the pilothouse."

We opened the cabin doors, one after another, and looked in. It felt as if we were opening tombs. Each stateroom sat in heavy silence, with a red plush chair pulled up to a marble-topped table and rosy light pressing through stained glass at the top of the windows.

Grandpa's cabin was far forward and easy to spot. There was a speaking tube hung on the wall, a brass bed, Grandpa's pilot's license framed near the door, and baby pictures of Glorietta and me. There was also one of Ma as a young girl and another of Ma and Pa together.

Still, the room looked ransacked and the bed looked freshly slept in. We didn't find the logbook, but Glorietta discovered a club under the bed. A bur-oak club.

She gave me an anxious glance. No doubt about it, the Fool Killer had been sleeping in Grandpa's brass bed.

Ma opened the window to air out the cabin.

We climbed the stairs to the top deck. The pilothouse sat like a box of windows to the rear of the black smokestacks. But there wasn't a scrap of paper to be found inside. Not even Grandpa's river charts.

Ma shook her head. "What *had* he been doing, steaming off out of the main river!"

"Fool Killer!"

"Hang'm! Bash'm!"

Both Ma and Glorietta looked up in surprise. I'd forgot to tell them about those spooky ol' crows. They'd flocked onto the crown of the smokestack again.

"Ravens!" Glorietta exclaimed.

"Just common crows," I said.

"Same kin," Ma remarked. "I wonder who taught them to speak."

"Maybe it was Grandpa," I said. "Those birds keep worryin' Shagnasty John. The Fool Killer, too. They keep chunking rocks at them."

We kept searching for papers. The ship's log must be somewhere. And there might even be a letter or two Grandpa had meant to send off to us.

I ended up poking around on my own. The freight deck was piled to the guardrails with stacks and stacks of milled lumber and windows and barrels of nails. I explored around and ended up at the door of the engine room. I turned the brass knob and looked in. I could make out the huge furnace and the white-faced steam gauges and the brass tubing gleaming in the shadows. I edged inside and gazed all around. Almighty clean, the engine room, I thought. There wasn't even the feel of grit under my shoes.

I was starting back outside when I whirled about. A faint rustling sound had caught my ear.

"Who's there?" I said quickly.

I peered into the gloom and waited, but no one answered. Something had moved, but I couldn't make out a thing. Maybe a rat, I thought. Ma would have a perishing fit if she thought there were rats underfoot, and I didn't much like the idea myself. I scrambled out of there and shut the door.

Pa and the outlaws returned with our trunks and sacks of dry food and Mr. Johnson and the chickens and the heavy printing press and all the newspaper stuff. They had fixed boat poles to the sides of the horses like wagon shafts and had dragged everything through the weeds on rough platforms of lumber lashed together. In my Quickshot Billy stories I'd read about Indians toting their belongings that way.

"Colonel," Shagnasty John said, wiping his face with his bandanna. "If I was you I'd camp right here in the cottonwoods."

"Nonsense. There's good shelter aboard the boat."

"I'm downright anxious to be up and gone. We made an agreement, didn't we? Shook on it, too. You don't want to pack all this plunder aboard."

"Of course I do."

Shagnasty John flashed the Fool Killer an uneasy look. Then he turned his eyes back to Pa, who was handing me a couple of Ma's flowerpots.

"I'm thinking of the women and children, Colonel," said Shagnasty John. "They won't like sleeping even one night aboard that cussed riverboat. No sir."

"What are you talking about?"

Shagnasty John's gaze seemed to float off somewhere. Almost under his breath, the Fool Killer said, "Can't nobody sleep much."

Shagnasty John was clearly embarrassed to tell what was on his mind. Finally he spit to one side and said, "No one tougher'n me and the Fool Killer. Ain't scared of nothing. But you'll never print up that newspaper for us. Not on the boat."

Pa said, "I gave you my word, sir."

"It's the woman and children, Colonel. They'll be too scared. That's the truth."

"Nonsense."

"Wait'll you hear them peculiar sounds that come in the night," Shagnasty John said. "And things'll disappear. And those blasted crows'll start calling out *your* name. I tell you, Colonel, it was all me and Fool Killer could do to stay hid out here. That boat has a ghost aboard. And that's a fact. It's haunted."

9

The Sheriff of Sunrise

PA SET UP his printshop in a rear cabin. The boat haunted?
"Flap-jawed foolishment," he declared. And Ma said, "I'd
sooner have a ghost aboard than those two high-smelling
ruffians."

She gave Mr. Johnson and the chickens the run of the
freight deck. I thought about the sounds I had heard in the
engine room. Maybe it *wasn't* a rat. Glorietta gave my
sleeve a tug. "Wiley, what if there is a ghost aboard?"

I tried to sound as certain as Pa. "Foolishment," I said.

"But Shagnasty John and the Fool Killer — they heard
him."

"One see is worth twenty hears," I answered.

The Fool Killer stood off by himself. He watched us
with his deep-socketed eyes as if he had found a whole
passel of fools.

Shagnasty John dusted off his hands after all the hauling about. "How long you figure to take printing us up
that newspaper?"

"You'll have it tomorrow," Pa answered.

Ma said, "Mr. Shagnasty — or whatever it is you call
yourself — you or your friend must have seen the ship's
logbook somewhere."

"Reckon we did," said Shagnasty John.

Ma's eyes lit right up. "That's splendid. Where is it?"

"I burnt it," the Fool Killer answered in that quiet voice of his.

"Burned it!"

"Yes, m'am," Shagnasty John nodded. "Every scrap of paper we could lay hands on. To start up our cook fires — when we had grub to cook. I tell you that ghost is meaner'n galvanized sin — even stole the last of our coffee beans. If we didn't sleep with our hardtack the creature'd have stole that too. Me and Mr. Fool Killer ain't had a square meal in so long, m'am, it's a wonder we don't throw shadows with holes where our stomachs used to be. That goose looks mighty mouth-watering."

"Don't you dare lay a hand on Mr. Johnson!" Ma snapped. "I'll pick out a couple of chickens."

"And Fool Killer would consider it a pleasure to twist their necks for you."

Ma gave them a suffering look. "You're not going to sit down to supper with us without a clean bath. Both of you."

Shagnasty John gave Ma a sulky squint. "M'am, you misjudge us. We bath regular. Every Fourth of July."

"I'll cut you a piece of soap," Ma said firmly.

"Ain't more'n a drop of water aboard."

"There's plenty in the river. Wash your clothes while you're at it." And then Ma added, "Take some water kegs with you. When you get back you can wash windows."

Shagnasty John grumbled in his beard, but before long he and the Fool Killer rode off toward the river. They both looked as out-of-sorts and cantankerous as freshly sheared sheep.

"Rufus," Ma said in the printshop. "What in merciful powers have you hatched up with those two?"

Pa had hung up his coat and was unbuttoning his vest. "I promised them one edition of a newspaper. Let's see — we'll need a name for the masthead. And we'll all have to get busy on it."

"What on earth do they want with a newspaper?" Ma scoffed. "I'll bet it takes both of them to read one sentence."

Pa gazed thoughtfully at a tray of large maplewood letters. "It's perfectly simple. We're going to print the news that Shagnasty John and the imposter who calls himself the Fool Killer were caught, tried, and hung right here in Sunrise. How about calling our newspaper *The Humbug Mountain Hoorah*? Yes, *humbug* strikes just the right note."

"But *Hoorah* for what, Pa?" Glorietta asked.

"Once the ink is dry we'll be shed of the terrors of the plains." Pa began plucking the blocks of wooden type. "I persuaded them to ride out and leave the papers in barbershops and aboard steamboats and around general stores. News that they've been hung is bound to make the telegraph wires. The law will stop looking for them. And they won't have to hide out *here* any longer."

Ma gave a huge sigh of relief, and smiled. "Hoorah!"

"Of course, those two have got reserved seats in hell," Pa added. "They're bound to be recognized by some sheriff or other when they try to hand out this humbug."

63

Pa arranged the blocks of type on our marble composing stone, and we all looked at the masthead. The letters were stacked backward so that they'd print forward, but we all could read backward.

"Wiley," Pa said. "We'll need a fearless lawman to arrest them. You've just been elected sheriff of Sunrise."

"Me?" I answered, startled.

"Daring capture in broad daylight. I'll write the story myself."

10

The Face in the Mirror

SHAGNASTY JOHN and the Fool Killer washed windows, and when they finished Ma put them to work cleaning up the cabin deck. They scowled and frowned and muttered between themselves. I do believe they were more anxious to be shed of Ma than we were of them.

Pa began clacking letters into his typestick, composing the capture news as he went along. Hardly without interrupting his train of thought he told us to think up stories to fill out the columns. After all, *The Humbug Mountain Hoorah* had to look enough like a real newspaper to fool Shagnasty John and the Fool Killer.

"If Wiley gets to be sheriff," Glorietta protested, "what about me?"

"You can be premier singer at the Sunrise Opera House. Mademoiselle Glorietta, the internationally famous songbird of the prairies."

Glorietta turned up her sharp, freckled nose. "I can't sing, Pa. I'd rather be dogcatcher."

"There are no dogs in Sunrise."

"There's no opera house, either."

"All right, we'll make you the first lady pilot of the Missouri steamboat *Phoenix*. Yes, that'll make a splendid news item."

Even though it was all make-believe, I must confess I felt inches taller to be sheriff. I supposed I ought to investigate the engine room again, but I knew Pa wouldn't let me carry his pepperbox pistol.

I waited until we were alone, and told him that if it wasn't a rat, well, there was *someone* hiding down there. And keeping the machinery slick and clean.

"It could be the haunt Shagnasty John told us about," I said.

"I never heard of a ghost cleaning and dusting," Pa laughed. "More nonsense, Wiley. But come on. It could be your grandfather."

I felt a surge of hope. Pa led the way. Once below, he threw open the engine-room door. He spied a square lantern hanging from a wall bracket, took it down, and struck a match to it. Pa appeared a bit surprised that there was enough oil in it to catch and light up.

He held it high as we poked through every corner of the engine room. But nothing showed itself. Nothing rustled. Nothing moved.

Pa ran a finger along a valve rod. "It's been wiped down with oil," he said, rubbing and feeling it between his thumb and fingertip. "Mighty strange."

"It must be Grandpa!" I exclaimed.

"I doubt it. I've never known your grandfather to hide from anyone. He's pitched bigger ruffians than these two off his boat."

Pa gave the machinery a final glance, blew out the lantern, and hung it up.

"Whoever is here, isn't here now," he said.

Shagnasty John and the Fool Killer slicked down their hair before coming in to supper. Pa had lit the chandelier and we had all beat dust out of the faded red-velvet dining-room chairs. And Glorietta was wearing her lost gold locket.

Ma had discovered it in the craw of one of the chickens. The hen had pecked it up way back in Mulesburg.

"M'am, I've eaten beaver, lizard, and coyote," Shagnasty John said, eating with both hands. "But this fried chicken beats all!"

He gorged down drop biscuits whole. The Fool Killer cracked a chicken foot between his teeth and sucked the bones dry.

After a thunderous slurp of coffee, Shagnasty John said, "I expect you folks'll be up and gone shortly. Can't say I blame you. Nothing around here but this boat, and it ain't worth ten cents of God-help-you."

"It'll do for the time being," said Pa.

Shagnasty John gave the Fool Killer the merest sideways glance, and I barely caught a flicker of something secret between them. Every time the Fool Killer looked up from his plate, which was hardly at all, it was as if he reckoned us fools overripe for his bur-oak club.

"Miss Glorietta, pass back the biscuits," Shagnasty John said in a merry tone of voice.

Glorietta glowered. "You're eating them all."

"Am I? I declare, my dear."

"I'm not your dear."

"Well, spare me one more. Make it two or three. They tickle the throat something grand."

I'd begun fooling with my mirror ring, glancing behind

me at the wood-paneled wall and the fanlights of colored glass over the windows. I wondered what Quickshot Billy Bodeen would do if he were sitting in the main cabin with two ornery outlaws. Oh, he'd crack their heads together, I thought, and toss them in jail and be back for dessert. And if there wasn't a jailhouse handy, he'd build one.

Suddenly my heart jumped a mile. The mirror ring caught the reflection of someone outside the window. I thought I glimpsed a face looking in, white as moonlight. I twisted my head and looked again. If my hair wasn't standing on end, it felt like it.

The window stood dark and empty.

Wasn't anyone at the table paying attention? Hadn't anyone seen the face! I looked across the table at Shagnasty John and the Fool Killer. If they'd seen anything they weren't letting on.

The haunt? But I didn't believe in ghosts, did I? I sat still, waiting for my breath to return and for the sudden coat of frost to melt off my skin.

I sat for a long time wondering what to do. Ma returned from the galley with dried-apple dessert. Maybe it had been the smell of hot food that lured the thing out of hiding. But haunts don't have to eat, I thought.

I looked at Pa. He'd be sorely disappointed in me if he thought I believed in ghosts. For certain it wasn't Grandpa I had seen. He'd have come roaring right in.

I kept my mouth shut. But by time dinner was over, I had managed to snitch a chicken wing and two biscuits, wrapping them in the napkin on my lap. I'd find out if I'd seen a haunt or not.

Ma began collecting dishes off the table, and when she

got around to Shagnasty John and the Fool Killer she said, "You two wash the dishes."

Shagnasty John's cheeks flamed up like a prairie fire. "M'am, you're talking to desperate, no-souled, man-killing, bank-robbing outlaws! Apron work is not in our line!"

"It is tonight," Ma said firmly.

"Doggone it, lady! That's goin' too far! We ain't had a wink of sleep all day the way you been ordering us around."

"And tomorrow you can polish the brasswork."

I managed to slip outside. I waited for my eyes to get used to the darkness. Clouds had drifted in and there wasn't a speck of starlight.

My heart thumping again, I felt my way to the stairs. I tried to imagine that I really was the sheriff of Sunrise and afraid of nothing. I slipped down to the freight deck and waited a moment, peering into the darkness all around me. It was not far to the engine room. I opened the door. The room was black. A team of oxen couldn't have dragged me inside.

I left the food just inside the door, and was quick getting myself back to the others. If the food was gone in the morning, there was a white-faced creature aboard — and hungry enough to come out of hiding. If the food was still in place, I reckoned, my mirror ring had caught sight of a genuine ghost.

By the time I returned, Shagnasty John and the Fool Killer had gathered up their bedrolls and belongings. They weren't going to stay aboard to wash dishes and polish doorknobs. They were going to bed down in the cottonwoods. They went marching across the gangplank.

70

The Fool Killer had fetched his bur-oak club and carried it on his shoulder.

Ma was smiling. "I thought I'd never persuade them to move off the boat."

11

The Humbug Mountain Hoorah

GREAT GUSTS of rain in the night rattled the pilothouse windows. Earlier in the day I'd announced I wanted to sleep in the wheelhouse and Ma had let me take my blankets up there. I wished I could change my mind when it came dark, but I didn't want to appear a coward.

I can't say I slept much. Broadsides of rain kept waking me. I thought about Shagnasty John and the Fool Killer. I imagined them stretched out in the mud and cussing the downpour. They might have come whimpering back aboard, like wet dogs, but I reckoned they were too proud and ornery for that. Or they were glad to be shed of the haunt aboard.

I felt scared myself and did wish I'd slept in one of the cabins, near Ma and Pa and Glorietta. I was glad when morning broke. By then the storm had tailed off, passing east over the prairie.

I watched through the windows for a while. With the *Phoenix* sunk to the bottom I couldn't look over the tops of the trees. But in the other direction I could see forever, and if I didn't know better I'd think the world was flat.

I stepped out onto the wet deck and didn't lose much time ankling down to the engine room. I took a turn on the brass knob and opened the door. The napkin lay neatly folded.

But the food was gone.

I stared at things. It wasn't rats who had got at the chicken and biscuits. Rats couldn't fold a napkin any more than a ghost.

No sir! Neither one. There was someone hiding aboard.

When I told Pa, he lowered his eyebrows thoughtfully. He said not to worry Ma and Glorietta about my discovery. A stranger aboard, prowling around at night, was enough to make anyone jumpy. Whoever it was, Pa calculated, he must have his own reasons for keeping himself out of sight. "Leaving a bit of food was clever of you, Wiley. That man's shy as a rabbit. When he discovers we mean him no harm it won't surprise me if he turns up big as life."

Shagnasty John and the Fool Killer kept to the cottonwoods. Pa, with the pepperbox pistol in his coat pocket, himself carried them a pot of coffee and breakfast beans.

We spent the morning setting type and making up the pages of the newspaper. Ma pecked letters from the type drawer almost faster than the eye could follow. She said she was writing about "the Incredible Talking Crows of Sunrise." Glorietta, at a different typecase, wouldn't say what she was up to. But she was smiling and humming to herself.

I held an empty typestick in my left hand, thinking awhile. Then I began setting a column inch or two about the gold locket found in the craw of the chicken. But I ran out of the letter *k* so I left out the word *locket*. I reckoned it didn't matter; *The Humbug Mountain Hoorah* wasn't a real newspaper with real news.

Every so often Shagnasty John yelled up from the cottonwoods. "Mornin' folks! Ain't our newspaper ready yet?"

Pa ignored him.

As our typesticks filled up, we transferred the lead letters to the composing stone. Pa had laid out two chases — cast-iron frames the size of the page — and with all of us setting type, the news columns grew fast.

Pa plugged up leftover space with advertisements he made up on the spot. With a maple block and mallet he leveled the type for printing and locked up the front page. He clamped the chase on the press and inked up the roller while the rest of us were still busy setting the back page.

The Humbug Mountain Hoorah was going to be a single sheet, the size of a handbill, printed on both sides. Fifty copies, Pa said, would be enough. We didn't have paper to squander.

"Afternoon!" Shagnasty John called up. "What's keepin' you folks? Me and Fool Killer are rarin' to travel!"

When the newspapers came off the press, we stood around reading all the foolishment we had set in type. Ma shook her head and laughed. "No one with an ounce of sense is going to believe a word of it."

GREAT EXCITEMENT!
Outlaws Captured!

Shagnasty John and
the Fool Killer Tried,
Sentenced, and Hung!

Terrors of the Prairies
Get their Necks Stretched.

Sheriff Wiley Flint makes
daring, single-handed
arrest in Sunrise!

Pa filled two columns and a half with this brand of moonshine. I felt kind of embarrassed, but it was almost like reading a Quickshot Billy story. At the end Pa wrote:

> After justice was done, the citizens of Sunrise showed admirable compassion for the departed desperadoes. Tombstones made of solid blocks of ice were set over their graves.
>
> "They'll need all the melted ice water they can get, where they're going," explained Mr. Johnson, the justice of the peace.

Pa didn't mention that Mr. Johnson was a bull goose. Ma had finished her story with the claim that the Incredible Talking Crows spoke the King's English better than anyone else in the territories and were available for elocution lessons. Glorietta's story announced that Ma had just been elected mayor of Sunrise. Ma gave a little shriek of laughter when she read that.

When we had finished, Pa yelled down to the cotton-woods. "Come get your obituaries!"

I don't know how Shagnasty John had fished the pepper-box pistol out of Pa's coat pocket.

He came aboard, all smiles and friendliness, with the Fool Killer ambling along behind. They tracked muddy footprints on deck.

Pa handed over the stack of newspapers. "The ink's still wet," he said. "But you'll see that I kept my word. Good day, gentlemen."

"Well, not quite so fast," Shagnasty John grinned. "Me and Fool Killer wouldn't want to be taken advantage of, Colonel. We'll just study it a bit and make sure you got it right."

He licked his thumb, dealt off a single copy of *The Humbug Mountain Hoorah,* and shifted it back and forth in front of his nose until his eyes got the focus. Squinting hard, he commenced to read about the capture in a mumbling voice. He stumbled considerably and leaped over some words entirely. "Colonel," he said, interrupting himself, "some of them paragraphs are thorny as a cactus patch. What is that pesky long word that keeps cropping up — *S-h-a-g-n-a-s-t-y?*"

"That's your name," Pa said, impatiently.

"I declare! I never saw it wrote out before."

It took him so long I must have grown an inch before he got to the end. "Fool Killer," he roared. "It says in white and black you and me are guaranteed dead — had our necks stretched at the end of a rope. Now, don't that cheer you up? Ain't nothing going to follow us now but our own shadows."

The Fool Killer barely shrugged. His deep eyes fixed us with double-barreled shots of darkness.

"We're much obliged, Colonel," Shagnasty John exclaimed. He rolled up the stack of newspapers and stuck them into a deep pocket of his bearskin coat. When his hand came out — there was the pepperbox pistol.

He spread his legs firmly, pointed the gun at us, and he wasn't smiling anymore. "Colonel, we weren't born in the woods to be bit by a fox. Directly we're gone you'll flap your coattails and inform the law that this here story is a bamboozle. Ain't that so, Fool Killer?"

The Fool Killer began to grin. Wider and wider. I remembered now the secret look the outlaws had traded at supper the night before. They'd had this in mind all along!

Pa straightened to his full height and viewed the men with such a wintery blast they ought to have suffered frostbite. "I had no such intention," Pa said. "I see now that I misjudged you. I credited you with common intelligence. Smart enough to take full advantage of a man's word and handshake. It's clear now that one of you doesn't have the brains God gave geese, and the other is wearing a seven-dollar hat on a five-cent head."

I looked up at Pa, all my muscles gone taut, and wished he'd held back on that volley of insults. They'd be flea-hopping mad.

"We'll consider them your final and last words, Colonel," said Shagnasty John, glowering. "Don't you know straight up when you see it? I'm holding the gun, sir! And we can't have the pack of you on the loose, knowing what you know. That's commonsensical."

"Nonsensical," Pa snapped.

"I told you to shut your jaws!" Shagnasty John turned to the Fool Killer. "You take 'em into the woods. One or two at a time."

All the Fool Killer's yellow teeth were showing now. "With my gnarly club?"

"Of course, with your gnarly club! Can't waste ammunition, can we? We're going to need every drop of lead, ain't we? Start with the shirttail boy and the girl."

The crows were squawking overhead, their black shadows flapping like bats along the deck. Pa's nostrils were all but giving out steam now, and I knew he was calculating the best moment to spring at Shagnasty John. The moment he had in mind must have been when the Fool Killer grabbed me and Glorietta.

But that was the moment a voice cut through the air, sharp as an ax. It came from the roof of the top deck.

"You! Drop the gun! I've got your overblown nose in my sights."

Our heads jerked upward. A skinny man stood tall against the sky, a rifle aimed downward, one of his eyes snapped shut and the other peering along the sights. His face was white as a mushroom.

Shagnasty John stood awestruck. You'd think he was looking at a ghost, and maybe he thought he was.

"If I squeeze this trigger another hair, mister, you'll have an extra hole for breathing." The man's voice was steady as his aim. "I recommended you drop that beanshooter, didn't I?"

Shagnasty John seemed to come unfroze. "Fixin' to, yes sir." He squinted up at the man. "You the varmint that's been haunting this boat? Ain't sociable to do a thing like that! Why, Fool Killer's been gooseflesh from toe to head."

"Drop it!"

"Yes indeedy, sir!" Shagnasty John let the pepperbox clatter to the deck.

"Pick it up, Colonel," said the man.

Pa nodded grandly and gathered up his pistol. Ma gave a quick sigh of relief. "Get your hands off my children," she snapped at the Fool Killer.

He dropped us like poison ivy, and we scrambled over to Pa and Ma.

The man on the roof kept his open blue eye to the sights. "Now then, you mildewed, lop-eared, flea-bitten buzzards — let's see if you can run for your horses quicker'n I can shoot. And don't stop running until you're out of the territory. Get gone!"

The outlaws made a footrace along deck and about tripped each other trying to be first onto the gangplank. They bounced across. I could hear Shagnasty John chuffing like a steam engine. The Fool Killer threw a glance back over his shoulder. He looked mad enough to bite nails.

Before long they whipped their horses out of the cottonwoods and headed for the setting sun.

Pa slipped the pepperbox pistol back into his pocket. "There's coffee on the stove," he said, tossing a look up at the stranger. "We'd be highly honored if you'd join us —"

But the man was gone.

12

Mr. Slathers

IT DIDN'T take Pa long to figure a way to smoke the man out of hiding. He kept a pot of coffee boiling on the stove while we busied ourselves in the printshop. We had to distribute the newspaper type back into drawers, letter by letter, being careful to toss each into its own small compartment. The powerful smell of coffee drifted to every quarter of the boat.

Ma set an extra place for supper, and Pa said, "Leave the door open."

We sat at our places and waited a good ten minutes or more. The doorway remained dark and empty. The stranger was almighty strange, I thought.

"You *sure* it wasn't Grandpa?" Glorietta asked.

"I would certainly recognize my own father," Ma said. "Well, there's no point in letting supper turn cold. It doesn't look like he's going to join us."

Pa nodded and we began passing around platters. "Confound it! I'll be sorry to leave without thanking the man."

Ma shot a startled look at Pa. "Leave? It's a roof over our heads, Rufus."

"As Shagnasty put it, there's nothing out here worth ten cents of God-help-us. It appears he was right. And our food won't last another week, Jenny."

"We can catch fish, Pa," I said. "And maybe jack-rabbits."

"Can't we stay longer?" Glorietta exclaimed. "I've got a whole room to myself. And Grandpa —"

"He's gone," Pa said. He avoided Ma's eyes. It was almost as if he was thinking that Grandpa might even be dead. But what he said was: "It's a wide country and we haven't a clue where to look for him. I'm truly sorry. There's nothing to hold us in Sunrise. We can't make a living out of weeds and jackrabbits."

"We could collect buffalo bones!" Glorietta cried out. "Captain Cully said he'd pay good money for 'em."

I perked up at the idea. But I couldn't help saying, "Glorietta, you said you'd rather *perish* than collect buffalo bones." I turned to Pa. "Could we?"

But Pa was no longer listening. He was gazing at the doorway. We stopped talking.

The stranger had appeared.

His hair was watered down and parted in the center, and he wore an old dark blue coat with brass buttons. I stared at him. We all stared at him. He was barefoot and seemed to have the dry wilts like the Fool Killer and almost everything else around Sunrise.

"Slathers's my name," he muttered. "I brought my own tin mug. If I could have the borrow of a cup of coffee I'd be downright obliged."

"Certainly not," Ma said, quickly gathering her wits. "Not unless you join us for supper. A place has been set, Mr. Slathers."

He held back. I'd never seen a grown man so overcome by the bashfuls. He looked like he didn't know where to get. Finally he said, "I'm mostly used to eating alone, m'am. I probably forgot my table manners. I never was one for the fuss and feathers of company."

"Mr. Slathers, do come in," Ma declared, smiling. "We're plumb out of fuss and feathers. Just corn fritters and common doings."

Like a puff of wind he was gone.

Pa gazed at the empty doorway and shook his head. "He appears to be a cast-iron hermit. I wonder if that brass-button ship's coat is really his own."

The room fell silent. I reckon each of us was thinking the same thing. If Mr. Slathers belonged to the *Phoenix,* he'd know a thing or two about Grandpa.

"His hair was slicked down and all," Ma said. "He wanted to be sociable."

"He's hungry," Pa said. "That's certain."

Ma rose from her chair. "I'll find him. I've *got* to talk to him, Rufus."

As suddenly as he had vanished Mr. Slathers reappeared in the doorway. He cleared his throat softly, two or three times. And I noticed he'd pulled on shoes. "I don't suppose you'd have any use for this sorry old can of peaches," he stammered.

"I love peaches!" Glorietta blurted out.

"Bring them right in, Mr. Slathers," Ma said. "How thoughtful of you! Peaches for dessert — I declare!" She accepted the can from his hands. "Sit right there between Glorietta and Wiley."

He slipped into his chair.

"Howdy," I said.

"Hello," Glorietta said.

"Hello," he said.

"Howdy," he said.

Pa introduced Ma and himself, but he already seemed to know who we were. I reckoned he'd overheard a lot of talk with the outlaws. We got busy passing him the supper platters.

"You saved our lives and we're eternally in your debt, Mr. Slathers," Pa said.

Now that he was seated among us he seemed to thaw out, little by little. After a long moment he said, "It was neighborly of you to leave me that grub last night."

"That was Wiley's doing," Pa said.

"I been hiding inside the ship's furnace," Mr. Slathers remarked. "Those two cutthroats never thought to look there."

"Neither did we!" I exclaimed.

He smiled. "Thanks for the feed, Wiley. And m'am, these fritters are first-rate."

Mr. Slathers was turning friendly as a lamb. And talkative too, as if he'd stored up enough words to bust. He said he'd bunked down in the furnace months ago, when Shagnasty John and the Fool Killer first turned up. "They came aboard while I was over to Wolf Landing for supplies."

"Wolf Landing?" Pa asked, his interest aroused.

"Thirty miles upriver. The nearest town."

"Does it have a post office?"

Mr. Slathers nodded. I wished Pa wouldn't interrupt him that way. What difference did it make if there was a post office or not? "I got back here at night and those fools

84

began shooting at me," he went on. "They didn't see me. They were just shooting at noises. Mighty jumpy, those squatters. That's what gave me the idea."

"What idea?" Ma asked.

"I figured I'd just scare them off. I dislike having to drop an ounce of lead into a man." A smile flashed up into his eyes. "I'd mouse out of hiding when they were snoring, and mislay their boots and make off with their chewing tobacco. Anything else they didn't have bolted down. Even lifted their cartridges a few at a time until they were down to empty gunbelts. At first they thought one was stealing from the other. But it wasn't long before I heard the howling fools talking about ghosts. And the crows didn't ease their minds any."

"Was it you taught them to talk?" I asked.

Mr. Slathers nodded. "I did educate a couple of them. By gum, when the squatters heard their very own tarnacious names squawked in the air they were plumb mystified. Haunts and ghosts, haunts and ghosts — that was about all they talked about. But still they wouldn't clear out."

Pa said, "They must have been more scared of getting fly-trapped by the law than of your ghost."

"Likely," remarked Mr. Slathers. "But their heads rattled with schemes and plans. There's something peculiar due to come down the river from way up in Montana and they were trying to figure some way to lay hands on it. 'Two tons of dust!' Shagnasty would thunder out every so often. I don't know what's so tempting about two tons of dust."

"Well, there's certainly no shortage of dirt around here," Ma shrugged. "Heads as soft as goose grease, those two!"

I could tell from the pondering look in Pa's eyes that he didn't like this turn of events. "Did they say when they expected this odd cargo?"

"I don't think it much mattered. I overheard 'em once saying they'd need to be armed to the teeth. But they didn't even have a lump of lead to shoot the crows."

Mr. Slathers had cleaned every morsel off his plate, but he wouldn't take second helpings. Maybe he thought it was bad manners. Ma urged him to help himself, but in the end it was Glorietta who heaped his plate all over again.

"Thank you, Miss Glorietta," he said, kind of embarrassed. "I'm bound to confess I'm a mite hungrier than is polite." And then, looking at us around the table, he added, "You folks lost?"

"Not if this is Sunrise, the Parnassus of the West," Pa remarked. "Disappointed, yes. Confounded and perplexed — yes, again. But not lost, Mr. Slathers."

And Ma said, "We expected to be met by my father, Captain Tuggle." Hope flashed up in her eyes. "Do you know him, sir?"

Mr. Slathers's neck straightened like a maypole. "I declare — the captain's own kin! Why, m'am, I'm chief engineer of the *Phoenix*."

"Then you surely know what happened," Ma exclaimed. "Where is he?"

Mr. Slathers's ghostly pale face slackened. "A first-rate gentleman, your father," he said. "Poor old Captain Jack. The river keelhauled him."

Ma's eyes froze. She held her breath. "He's not drowned, Mr. Slathers? He's not dead?"

"The captain? No, m'am! Tougher'n an old lanyard knot is Captain Jack Tuggle. Gone, though."

"Gone where?"

Mr. Slathers avoided Ma's anxious eyes. "Wouldn't say. Headed up north, maybe. Or down south. Or east. Or west. He was so deep in the glooms, m'am, it didn't much matter."

"In the glooms?" Pa said. "What happened?"

"The spavined, muddy, cantankerous, misbegotten Missouri flooded, that's what happened. When the water settled, the river stood a mile off. It had cut itself a new channel. Left the *Phoenix* high and dry. You can see that."

"Yes," Ma said.

"Wasted a smart lot of dynamite trying to blast the river back where it belonged. But the Missouri's got a mind of its own. Sunrise went bust before it got fairly started. The captain's fine river lots are now too far from the Missouri to be worth a nickel."

"But a mile," Pa said, "hardly seems serious. A short walk."

Mr. Slathers shook his head. "A short walk, maybe, but a man could drown going to the nearest saloon."

"I certainly don't understand," Ma remarked.

Mr. Slathers waved an arm as if to take in all of Sunrise. "This grit used to be Dakota Territory. It's now Nebraska. The river is the dividing line."

"If I understand you," Pa said, leaning forward, "a

caprice of the river shifted Sunrise from Dakota Territory to Nebraska. What in Sam Hill have saloons got to do with it?"

"Heaps, Colonel. Knockemdead is legal in Dakota."

"Knockemdead?" Ma asked.

"Whiskey, m'am. Illegal on this side of the river. Nebraska has voted itself dry." Mr. Slathers swallowed a mouthful of food. "The first ventures of commerce in Sunrise were six tent saloons and more on the way. When the river jumped, those knockemdead fellows found themselves out of business. They packed their whiskey barrels and hauled anchor before the Nebraska law turned up. Before long there weren't enough men in town to build a horse trough. This far from civilization a man gets thirsty. The crew jumped ship with the rest."

"Except the chief engineer," Pa remarked.

"I was tempted," answered Mr. Slathers. "But I couldn't leave my boiler and valves and rods to rust away, could I? Still keep things oiled."

"Then you expect Captain Tuggle back!" Ma exclaimed.

"I about give up on that," Mr. Slathers mumbled. "It's goin' on two years."

There was a spell of quiet.

Mr. Slathers shifted uneasily in his chair. Then he said, "A quantity of the captain's friends bought his riverside lots, sight unseen. Just from the picture. His partners in St. Louis had that thing lithographed up. Captain Jack meant to make that picture good. Why, we got a ten-room hotel aboard, the lumber all cut to size, windows and all. A fine little opera house, too. Came from Chicago — Bridges

Ready-Made Houses. The captain paid cash. But Sunrise is never going to be now, and the captain's gone bust. Can't pay his friends back their money. Won't show his face. His partners disappeared with the cash."

I had been careful not to open my mouth, being all ears, but I said, "I reckon Grandpa's out tracking them down. I bet he is!"

"It crossed his mind. But he calculated they'd have the money spent before he could shake any greenbacks out of their pockets. No, he won't be back — not until he can pay off everyone or make good on the town. That's how it is with the captain."

Ma took a breath and looked at Pa. "We'll start packing. And start looking."

Mr. Slathers gave his head a shake. "M'am, his trail is dog-nose cold."

Pa was gazing off into space. Then he cocked his head, lifted an eyebrow, and smiled. "Simple. It's all very simple. We'll stay right here."

"What?" Ma said. "Rufus, we can *try* to find him."

Pa's smile broadened. "No need to. *He'll* find us."

"He will?" Glorietta said vaguely. She didn't understand any better than I, but we both knew when Pa had a surprise up his sleeve.

"Certainly!" He ripped out a laugh. "Those two useless outlaws don't know it, but they're going to be doing us a great service. Holy jumped-up Moses! They'll be handing out *The Humbug Mountain Hoorah,* won't they? Some folks won't have better sense than to swallow it whole. And that's bound to put Sunrise gloriously and firmly on the map. Yes, indeed — the city where the notorious Shagnasty John and the Fool Killer were caught, tried, hung, and buried. Word'll spread mouth to mouth. Sunrise, a thriving metropolis boasting that fearless lawman, Sheriff Wiley Flint. The Parnassus of the West, with its own justice of the peace and the first lady mayor. That's you, Jenny."

Glorietta's eyes lit up behind her glasses. "That was *my* idea!"

Pa exclaimed, "News of that nature is certain to find its way to Captain Tuggle — wherever he is."

"Merciful powers!" Ma said. She was smiling now too. "He's bound to come back."

"Quick as one-two-three," said Pa. He fished a couple of cigars out of his pocket and tossed one to Mr. Slathers. "Light up, sir."

And Ma said, "Mr. Slathers — will you join us in peaches for dessert?"

13

The Dead Man's Hand

IT WAS a couple of days later that Mr. Johnson discovered a dead man's hand.

By then Mr. Slathers had shown us that we could store water in the engine-room boiler. He and Pa stretched tarpaulins like awnings to catch rainwater from any passing downpour. It would beat hauling water an everlasting distance from the river. Ma set out her flowerpots. During the day she turned Mr. Johnson and the chickens loose in the cottonwoods to fend for themselves. It was our job to round them up before nightfall.

We didn't hang around much, Glorietta and me. We found a couple of potato sacks aboard and set out to collect buffalo bones. Four dollars a ton, Captain Cully had said. Cash money!

We followed the dry riverbed and pounced on anything bone white that caught our eyes. Mr. Johnson took to tagging along after us, and we were forever trying to chase him back. He'd give a honk and beat his wings, but a bull goose is hard to reason with. After a while we gave up on it.

Before long, buffalo ribs were sticking out of our sacks like sticks of bleached stovewood. Some of them we had to dig out with our bare hands, where grass had grown up over them.

"Wiley, how big a heap do you reckon it takes to make a ton?"

"I don't know," I said.

"What are you going to do with your share of the money?"

"Haven't given it a thought."

"Maybe I'll buy a piano. Ma'd like a piano."

"With two dollars!"

She shot me a defiant look. "I didn't say I was going to stop with one ton of bones, did I?"

"We get a piano, you'll have to practice. Me too, probably."

"I'd *like* to practice the piano."

"You're plumb addled," I said. It was likely Pa and Ma would need every cent. Their own money must be about gone, and it was bound to be a long wait for Grandpa to turn up.

We went scavenging all the way to the end of the old riverbed. The Missouri had thrown up acres of silt and a monstrous heap of dead logs before cutting itself a new channel.

We emptied our sacks near the river. That way it would be easier to load the stuff aboard the *Prairie Buzzard* when Captain Cully came steaming back.

Glorietta looked over our tangle of bones. "How much you figure we got?"

"It's a mighty puny pile," I answered. "A nickel's worth, maybe."

"That *all?*"

"We just started. What in tarnation do you expect?"

Mr. Johnson was eating grass grown up through a whole rack of buffalo ribs. We ambled over.

"What if Captain Cully steals our bone pile, Wiley? After we've got a big heap, I mean. Two or three tons maybe."

"He's shifty enough," I said. "We'll have to keep our eyes sharp."

"And why do you suppose Shagnasty John and the Fool Killer were in such a lather over two tons of dirt? *Dirt,* of all things!"

I tried to shoo Mr. Johnson out of the curved rack of ribs. "It doesn't make a thimbleful of sense to me."

"What's Mr. Johnson got?" Glorietta said. Then her voice jumped sky-high. "Wiley, there's a man buried here!"

I scurried around to her side of the tall bones.

A hand reached up out of the ground.

We stood frozen, both of us. The fingers were bent like a bird's claw. The whole hand looked kind of mummified. Mr. Johnson was still tearing away at the grass with his bill.

I chased him away with a stick and then poked the hand. Stiff as a dead branch.

"It *couldn't* be Grandpa," Glorietta said, glancing at me.

"Of course not," I declared. "Buried for ages, looks like."

"I don't want to touch it!"

"Then don't." I wasn't too anxious to touch the hand myself, but I began clawing out the dirt and weeds around it. Pretty soon I had scooped clear the whole, entire arm down to the elbow. I tapped it again. "Solid as a rock," I said.

"We'd better get Pa."

We left our sacks and ran. Mr. Johnson came honking after us.

Ma had strung up a rope in the sun and was hanging up a washing.

"Pa's not here," she said in a busy tone of voice.

"Mr. Johnson found a dead man!" Glorietta exclaimed. "Pa had better see it."

"Where'd Pa go?" I asked.

"Left for a while." Ma didn't even turn to look at us. "A dead man?"

"Turned hard as a rock," I said. Pa gone? It caught me up short and Glorietta, too. We always got that chill feeling whenever Pa left for anywhere. "Did he say when he'd be back?"

Ma turned and looked at us. "Children, there's nothing to worry about. We'll be safe enough. Pa left me his pepperbox."

"But where did he go?" Glorietta asked in a paper-thin voice.

"Well, now, we need supplies, don't we? You know that. Pa and Mr. Slathers decided to set out on foot for Wolf Landing."

"When'll he be back?" I asked. "Did he say?"

"No more than four days. You can count on it."

Of course we could, I told myself. Pa wouldn't disappear on us. He wouldn't leave us out here in the middle of nowhere. "Do you want to see our dead man?" I said.

"Heavens, no!" Ma exclaimed. "Certainly not."

14
Jim Chitwood

FOR ALL I KNOW Glorietta had been crying in her sleep. She came down with the dolefuls whenever Pa turned up missing. She didn't want to go bone-hunting the next day. She didn't want to go back to the dead man. She was just going to sulk around the boat, I guess.

"I'll go without you, then," I said.

"Go ahead."

"Doggone it, Glorietta, this isn't like the other times. He has Mr. Slathers along. And you heard what Ma said. They went for supplies."

"He could have taken us with him."

"A man doesn't have to tote around his whole family all the time," I said.

"He could have waited to say good-bye."

"He'll say hello when he gets back. Can't he get out of sight without you getting all fidgety? He's not tied to Ma's apron strings and he won't be tied to yours either. Grab your sack and let's go."

"You get fidgety too," Glorietta declared.

"I'm not a bit fidgety," I said, although that wasn't strictly the truth. You could never really be sure about Pa. "You coming?"

"No."

I left without her.

I kept my distance from the dead man for a couple of days. I just wandered about, and if Mr. Johnson wasn't following me it seemed that the crows were. Sack by sack the buffalo bones began to pile up, but I wished the days would go a little faster.

Every so often I passed the hand sticking up out of the ground and I tried not to look at it. A dead man wasn't exactly pleasant to have around, even if he had turned hard as stone. But I couldn't *help* looking at it, all grayish green and perishing old and with dirt clinging to it. When the grass was swaying in the wind I began to imagine I saw the hand move, as if that man was going to rise up out of the ground and shake himself off. It was spooky, that hand, and I finally dropped to my knees and buried it.

I spent a long time at the pilothouse windows on the day Pa and Mr. Slathers were due back. Ma had said they'd struck off due west instead of following the meanders of the river. Not a speck was moving toward us on the horizon. Finally I got my potato sack and left the boat.

It surprised me to find that Glorietta was already out bone-hunting. I reckoned she didn't want to be there when Pa got back. It was as if she would kind of be getting even with him a little. Maybe he'd think she was lost. Or even had run away.

When I met up with her, I didn't say anything and neither did she. We worked our way along the Missouri. Suddenly I hauled up short.

There was a birchbark canoe pulled up out of the water, and a man sitting on a buffalo skull.

"Where in damnation is Sunrise?" he ripped out, kind of mad-looking. He was a bandy-legged man with stuck-out ears, and he was wearing a fur cap.

"Sunrise," I said and pointed. "The city limits are right over there."

"I don't see anything but nothing *that* way. Or any which way. I been paddling up and down all morning."

"There's nothing in Sunrise but weeds and jackrabbits," I said.

"Well, where in damnation is the gold rush?"

I glanced at Glorietta and then back at him. "What gold rush?"

"The one I read about in the paper. First lump found in the craw of a chicken."

"But that was just a gold locket!" I said.

"This one," Glorietta declared. "The one I'm wearing."

He stood up. "Don't try to rumsquaddle me."

"Honest, mister," I said.

"I mean to stake my claim. Looks like I beat everyone else."

"More are coming?" I asked, dumbfounded.

"More? Hordes! You can count on it. I've got my pan and shovel. Just point me to the gold diggin's."

"Sir, it's all a mistake. You see —"

"I seen you two doing some prospecting yourselves."

"We're just digging buffalo bones."

"Horsefeathers! Jim Chitwood ain't likely to be taken in by a couple of shut-mouth young'uns. You know where that lump of gold was found!"

His voice wasn't entirely friendly. So I pointed toward the dry riverbed and said truthfully, "Over there."

"That's more like it," he said. We backed away. "Much obliged."

When we got back to the *Phoenix*, Mr. Slathers was there. But Pa hadn't returned with him.

"Locked himself up in a hotel room and wouldn't come out," Mr. Slathers said. "He asked me to see after you until he gets back."

15

The Diggings

A WHISTLING cold wind swept over the prairie for days on end. It set the tarpaulins flapping and the cabins to creaking. "Whipping down out of Canada," Mr. Slathers said cheerfully, "and not even a barbed wire fence to stop it."

He meant to look after us while Pa was away, and took it seriously. He sawed wood for the potbellied stove in the main cabin and kept a red-hot fire going. He showed me how to sharpen fishhooks and how to set a rabbit snare, but my mind wasn't on it. He didn't know about Pa and we tried not to let on. But he could tell we were all kind of edgy waiting.

"He'll be along, your pa," he said. And when the wind turned wet he said, "You don't expect the Colonel to slosh through all that downpour!"

The sky flashed and thundered, and the wind about took off the roof of the wheelhouse. Mr. Jim Chitwood scurried for cover from his harebrained gold-prospecting, and Ma rented him a cabin. The rain turned to great whistling balls of hail and a couple of other men turned up to warm themselves around the stove in the main cabin.

"Shucks, there's no gold strike around here," Mr. Chitwood scoffed at them. It appeared to me he was trying to deceive them into clearing out. But they didn't believe him any more than they did us. Ma rented them cabins, too.

"The *Phoenix* is turning into a regular hotel," she smiled. She seemed glad to be busy with things. Ma had a way of carrying her feelings locked up tight.

I kept pretty much to the pilothouse. During the worst of the storm it felt like being on a ship at sea. At times I couldn't see ten feet. I read my Quickshot Billy books all over again. But I was drawn back to the windows, hoping to catch a glimpse of Pa returning.

And then we woke up to clear, fresh skies. The earth began to steam under the sun. Mr. Chitwood lost no time making for his gold diggings. The other two men went dogging after him, and other strangers began turning up.

But not Pa.

I began to feel all thundery inside. How could he turn his back on us again? How could he be that way? Words I didn't want to think stormed about in my head. He was a cussed father. I didn't care a hoot if he never came back. Ever!

Glorietta wandered up to the pilothouse. We didn't say anything. One look and I could tell that she had been crying in her sleep again.

She spent a long time staring out the windows, due west. Finally, in a tight voice, she said, "Mr. Slathers wants to go back to Wolf Landing and fetch Pa. Ma won't let him. Let it be, she said. Why won't she let him? Is that what Pa does when he's gone? Locks himself up in a hotel room?"

"I don't know." I shrugged and picked up my potato sack. Did Pa think it was enough to palm us off on Mr.

Slathers? "It doesn't matter. We can get along without Pa."

I didn't know that Ma had come up and was standing in the doorway. "Wiley, don't say a thing like that."

I spun and red-hot anger spit out of me. "I hate him!"

Ma hardly lifted an eyebrow. She stood looking at us both and acting infernally calm. "Pa has his reasons. He'll turn up with a smile on his lips and a tip of his hat. That's the way it's always been. You know your father."

"No I don't!" I said. I threw the gunnysack over my shoulder and left.

We could make our living with buffalo bones, I told myself. Me and Glorietta and Ma. I dumped the sack and wandered about again to fill it up.

It wasn't long before a pack of men hailed me from a swiftly floating raft. They were looking for Sunrise. I guessed there was no use telling them about Glorietta's gold locket, but I tried and they just laughed.

With the weather cleared, it wasn't ten minutes before I saw another three men trudging about. A sudden idea all but lifted me out of my boots. If they were so anxious to start using their picks and shovels maybe they could dig the Missouri River back where it belonged — and refloat Grandpa's boat!

"Over that way," I called out, pointing. "At the end of the dry riverbed. Not a bit of gold, but that's where the other miners are digging."

All that day men kept flocking in, and I kept pointing them to the old riverbed. By the next day gold-seekers were turning up in heaps and hordes, just as Mr. Jim Chitwood said they would. Some of them had come with tents, but others had been in too much of a rush. Ma rented out every cabin on the *Phoenix*.

Mr. Slathers set out baited hooks every afternoon and in the mornings there'd almost always be a catfish or two to haul in. He showed me how to skin them. "Can't tell," he said. "Those fools in the dry bed might turn up another lump of gold. We had a deckhand picked himself up after a fight — lost a gold tooth."

The pile of bones was beginning to look like something. As often as not I'd find the crows sitting on top waiting for me.

"Fool Killer!"

"Hang'm!"

"Wiley!"

That caught me up short. Mr. Slathers! I thought. He'd taught the bull crow my name!

Every so often I'd stand at the dry riverbank and gaze at the men scrambling after gold. They swung picks in great arcs. Shovel loads of earth flew. Tents had sprung up along the bluffs like mushrooms after a rain. An army of men! And more rushing in from every direction.

One day Mr. Jim Chitwood, carrying his birchbark canoe over his head and shoulders like a tortoise shell, climbed the bluff and stomped past me.

"I'm clearing out," he said. "No blasted gold here."

"We tried to tell you," I said.

"Rumsquaddled!" he scowled.

He headed off toward the river. I was glad to see the last of that bandy-legged man with his stuck-out ears.

I went about my business. My gunnysack was about full and I headed for the bone pile. I reached the spot where the dead man was buried.

The hand was sticking up again.

It rose in plain sight and gave me a start. You'd think it had clawed its way out of the ground.

Only the rainstorm, I thought. Must be. The rain had washed away the loose dirt. I shouldn't let the thing spook me that way.

I dropped to my knees to cover it up again.

"*Wiley!*"

That bull crow, I thought, perched way off on the bone pile.

But the voice came again, closer this time, and not a crow voice at all.

"What you got there, Wiley?"

I turned. It was Pa, with a smile on his lips and a touch of his hat.

16

The Petrified Man

I GAVE PA a lightning flash of eyes and turned my back again. He'd been gone for eleven confounded days, but from his easy manner you'd think he'd only been out for a ten-minute stroll.

"That looks like a dead man," he said.

I picked up my heavy gunnysack and started away.

"Hold on, Wiley," he called softly.

"You're back. I can see that, sir."

"And you're angry. I can see that, too. I'd be surprised if you weren't."

I shrugged a little, my back still to him.

"I found another Quickshot Billy nickel novel over in Wolf Landing," he said. "It's kind of dog-eared and mouse-nibbled and not worth reading, but I thought you'd like to have it."

"You thought wrong." My insides were churning. I'd never talked to him that way before. "I'm too old for those infernal dumb stories anymore."

"I see. Ma tells me you and Glorietta have gone into the buffalo-bone business. Enterprising. That's mighty enterprising. I'm proud of you both, Wiley."

"I've got a mess of work to do," I said.

"And I don't mean to keep you. But I declare, Wiley,

that piece you wrote in *The Humbug Mountain Hoorah* certainly increased the population of Sunrise! All that amazing activity in the riverbed! I thought at first I'd come home to the wrong place. It wouldn't hurt if you turned around and looked at me. I'd be obliged, Wiley."

I took my time swinging around. I was trying to hang on to all my anger and at the same time trying to keep the water from rising to my eyes. "You needn't have rushed back for us," I said, doing my best to match his own loose and easy manner. "Hardly missed you. Me and Ma and Glorietta can take care of ourselves. We've done it before."

"Know that. Knew you could. It eases my mind, Wiley." He threw up the collar of his corduroy coat against the wind blowing off the river. "Truth is, your father's a shiftless, no-account, here-and-there sort of man. It pains me to admit it. I'm downright sorry."

That wasn't the truth. Not the whole truth, I thought. I stood glaring at him, and my ears felt crisp in the wind. He was being careful to dodge the real reason. He wasn't saying a word about locking himself in the hotel room. But I made the mistake of looking into his eyes, kind of wet but holding steady on me, and the stove-hot anger inside me began to cool.

"I don't much enjoy the sight of that dead hand," he said with a sudden grin. He was clearly glad to change the subject.

I took a long breath. "I didn't say you were no-account. Didn't think it, either."

"That man was thrown into an uncommonly shallow grave."

"Or shiftless, either."

108

"We ought to bury him properly."

I tried to wipe my nose on my sleeve without appearing to. "That man's solid as stone."

"You don't say."

I dropped the sack and tapped the dead hand with a stick. Pa cocked an ear to the hard sound.

"Stiffer'n a goose on ice," he said. "I declare."

He began scooping away the earth and pretty soon I was right there helping him. We uncovered a narrow, old face with shut eyes and hollow cheeks.

I said, "Looks like it could be an Indian."

"Might be." Pa snapped a finger against the man's sharp chin. Then he looked over at me. "Mummified."

"I expect so."

"Do you know what you found?"

"It was Mr. Johnson who found him first."

Under the knife-edge hat brim, Pa's eyes were alive with excitement. "Wiley, we'll have to publish another edition of *The Humbug Mountain Hoorah*. A story like this could be the making of Sunrise. Those misled gold-seekers will pack up one of these days soon, but other folks will come flocking."

"To look at a scruffy old mummy?"

"It's not a mummy," Pa said. "Must have been buried for an eternity, this man. And turned to stone. Wiley, what we're looking at is a *petrified man!*"

17

"Sinners Only"

It was a week before we got out the next issue of *The Humbug Mountain Hoorah*. First we had to dig up the petrified man.

"Careful, careful now," said Mr. Slathers as we pried the creature out of his grave. "We don't want the gentleman breaking like a vase."

"Remarkable," Pa said. "Not even a toe missing."

The petrified man was no taller than Glorietta. Not even as tall as I, it appeared to me. But he *was* monstrously heavy. We bundled him up in canvas and Mr. Slathers lashed him to a pair of long boat poles. It took hours to drag him to the *Phoenix,* and it was a mighty struggle to get him aboard. All Glorietta and I could do was try to steady him. It would be awful if he broke now.

"Aft on the cabin deck's a good place for him," Mr. Slathers said, and that's where they laid him out. Ma came over to have a look. "Horrors," she muttered.

"It's a great scientific discovery," Pa said.

"Well, don't expect me to keep him dusted."

It wasn't long before the miners sleeping aboard took to striking matches on his stone foot to light their pipes.

"That won't do," Pa said. "Wiley, with the cabins full I think you're going to have to share the pilothouse."

"With *that?*" I exclaimed, shooting a look at the creepy, dead-cold figure.

"I'll admit he's not going to be the most sociable companion. On the other hand, he won't keep you awake snoring. And he'll be safe. An aborigine, from the looks of him. Might be two, three thousand years old."

"We can cover him with a sheet," Glorietta said.

I tossed her a glance. I didn't want her to think the sight of that ancient dead man rattled me. "Oh, it's just a hunk of stone," I said. "No need to cover him."

It took ropes and all of us pulling to haul the mighty weight of him up the stairway. Once inside the pilothouse Pa and Mr. Slathers stood the petrified man at a corner window so I wouldn't trip over him in the dark. His eyes were tight shut, like someone asleep. Even then it was as if he were gazing out at the miners in the dry riverbed tearing up the earth. I wondered what thoughts had turned to stone in his head.

"Colonel," said Mr. Slathers. "If we could get some of those men to help us we've got cut lumber aboard for a ten-room hotel. Give some of the poor fools out there a roof over their heads."

But the miners were in such a gold fever that none of them was willing to lay down his pick and shovel and lend a hand. Pa and Mr. Slathers and Glorietta and I began toting lumber and rolling kegs of nails ashore.

The trouble was, Shagnasty John and the Fool Killer had burned the blueprints.

"It's going to take some doing to figure out what goes where," said Mr. Slathers. "And they burned up sticks of lumber with the blueprints. Pieces of the hotel are going to turn up missing."

We meant to start with the hotel, but it turned out to take on more of the shape of an opera house. Pa and Mr. Slathers kept sorting through the lumber and started another building.

"I do believe this piece belongs to the hotel," Pa said.

"If it fits, nail it down."

Glorietta and I helped try to sort out the puzzle of studs, windows, and doors. Ma too, when she and Pa weren't setting type for the newspaper. But it wasn't long before Mr. Slathers stood back to study the two buildings going up.

"Colonel, I think we've got a hotel that's part opera house, and an opera house that's part hotel."

Pa tipped back his hat. "Opera house," he muttered. "Then there must be an asbestos curtain to go with it."

"Of course there is. All rolled up."

"Fine. Splendid!" I knew the look in Pa's eyes. Some rollicking idea had come to him. "I've a two-inch hole to fill in the newspaper. And I know just how to fill it."

With fourteen miners sleeping aboard and taking breakfast and supper with us, Ma was running out of food again. It was mostly catfish every day. I'm certain we snared a rabbit now and then, but the men living along the riverbank stole them out from under us. Ma's chickens might have disappeared too if she hadn't penned them up on the freight deck. Mr. Johnson, too. The idea of roast goose must have set many a mouth to watering. The only times

Ma marched them ashore to grub around was when we were hammering away at the hotel and opera house, and could keep an eye on them.

Glorietta and I hardly had a moment of time to add buffalo bones to our heap. But we did slip away occasionally.

"Must be near a ton by now," Glorietta said.

"A ton, easy. Maybe two."

"We'd better keep a sharp lookout for Captain Cully."

"Wear your specs," I said.

She bridled. "You wear 'em. There's nothing out here to see. Anyway, we ought to be able to *hear* Captain Cully. The *Prairie Buzzard* rattles up more noise than a peddler's load of teakettles."

Not a day went by but more gold-seekers turned up. They began arriving on steamboats heading upriver. News of that confounded lump of gold had shot to great distances. Those miners would skin me alive if they knew it was all because I had left out the word *locket*. Just one dratted word. Well, I'd *tried* to tell them.

I know that Ma was keeping an eye out for Grandpa with every new man who showed up. I imagined the way he'd probably lift his eyebrows and look at the dirt flying in the riverbed and say, "What in Sam Hill is going on here?"

I can't say that my first nights with the scruffy petrified man were exactly joyful. At least his back was turned, and after a while I got used to his dead-silent company. It beat listening to the crows.

"Sunrise, Home of the Great and Only Genuine Petrified Man," Pa announced one evening. "That's the way I'm printing it up. Bound to create a stir in the world. Why, so many folks will come for a sight of it we'll need a *hundred*-room hotel — and then some."

Mr. Slathers cleared his throat faintly. It had taken him a while to shuck all his hermit shyness, but ever since Pa had stayed away he'd got used to looking out for us. He warmed right up to it. I got the feeling he was kind of borrowing us as his own kin. "That ancient gentleman must have got washed down in a roaring flood," he said. "Looks to me like he must have been buried way back somewhere with limestone-water dripping down. All that sediment hardened him into solid limestone — that's the way I figure it." And then, almost without a pause, "I'll be going back to Wolf Landing in a day or so."

I shot a glance at Pa. Mr. Slathers looked at Ma.

"You'll need more than a backload of supplies if you're going to feed all these miners aboard."

"Yes," Ma said in a flat voice. Her eyes avoided Pa. Then she seemed to perk up. "Yes, of course, Mr. Slathers. A wagonload of supplies. There's money from the miner's room and board."

"I'll rent a wagon and fill it up."

I was still watching Pa and so was Glorietta. If he noticed us, he didn't let on. "While you're in Wolf Landing," Pa said, "I'd be obliged if you'd drop off some copies of *The Humbug Mountain Hoorah*. It would be a fine start for the Petrified Man."

I could feel all my muscles let loose. Pa was staying with us.

He added, "And would you see if the postmaster is holding a letter for me?"

The Petrified Man wasn't the only company I had in the pilothouse. There was the nickel novel Pa had brought back from Wolf Landing, and I had tried to ignore it. But now I read it.

It was called *Quickshot Billy on the Warpath,* and was all about the time he had tracked a desperate outlaw two thousand miles to the Mexican border. The badman got the drop on him while Quickshot was having a breakfast of hot chili peppers and took his guns. But that ruffian hadn't counted on Quickshot Billy's resourcefulness. With a chili pepper between his fingers like a slippery watermelon seed he'd squirted the fiery juice into the outlaw's eyes. "First time I ever enlisted the aid of a vegetable in capturing an outlaw," Billy remarked.

"I don't believe a word of it," Glorietta said when I told her the story.

"You don't know Quickshot Billy's quick and agile mind," I said. "Nor his steel-clad courage."

"A chili pepper!" She groaned and rolled her eyes.

There was no talking sense to Glorietta at times. I read the book all over again, and it was even better.

When Pa got the second issue of *The Humbug Mountain Hoorah* printed, Mr. Slathers left with twenty copies on the long walk to Wolf Landing. Glorietta and I wandered among the gold diggers and sold a quantity of newspapers. Pa had mentioned a lot of their names in a column of mining news, not bothering to mention that no one had found a flake of gold. But that didn't seem to discourage them. As far as I knew the only one who had given up was Mr. Jim Chitwood.

Pa used his largest wooden type to announce the finding of the Great and Only Genuine Petrified Man, but that didn't cause any stir among the miners.

I heard a man who everyone called Hogfat laugh. "A petrified chap wouldn't assay out at a penny a pound — unless he had gold teeth!" That's where their mind was.

But he and some other rough-looking miners turned up at the *Phoenix* that night. It wasn't the limestone man that brought them. They had found something of greater interest on the back page.

Pa had needed to fill space and had printed:

SINNERS ONLY

ASBESTOS COFFINS!

Men bound for Hades! Get measured for our exclusive asbestos-lined coffins. Fireproof! Guaranteed to see you through the hereafter without scorching a hair. Money-back guarantee! Don't delay. Supply limited.

SUNRISE COFFIN WORKS

Flint & Slathers, Props.

18

Mr. Slathers's Surprise

SUNSET was flaring up red as silk when Mr. Slathers rode into sight. He was driving a wagon heaped with groceries.

"Wiley! Glorietta!" he called out. I think it was the first time I ever saw his lean face in a total burst of smiles. "Brought you a cargo of candy. Licorice and sour balls. Hope that meets with your approval."

"I'm partial to licorice and sour balls, both!" I said.

"Me too, Mr. Slathers!"

He leaped from the wagon and moved around with a joyful step. He had a gift of garden seeds for Ma. He'd had only his engine-room machinery to look after before. Now there was us and he was enjoying himself hugely. And he did bring back a letter for Pa, but Pa just stuffed it into his coat without opening it.

It fell dark before we toted all the supplies aboard. Campfires sprang up all along the dry riverbank, and the sky was a vast sparkle of stars. Mr. Slathers never stopped smiling. I got the feeling he was all but busting with a secret.

He had brought half a box of cigars, and after supper he and Pa lit up. I kept watching Mr. Slathers, but maybe he was waiting for the right moment to spring his surprise. If he had a surprise.

"There are enough supplies to feed an army," Ma said. "You must have struck some hard bargains, Mr. Slathers."

"Did my best, and got the rest on credit."

Ma looked slightly stricken. "Dear me. We're not only flat broke again, but in debt."

"Only temporary," Pa said, puffing away. "Mr. Slathers, I'm not much of a carpenter. I hope you are."

"I've done my share, Colonel."

"Splendid. You may have noticed we're partners in the Sunrise Coffin Works."

"I did. Be glad to help. Not that there's anyone fool enough to turn up for an asbestos coffin."

"So I thought," Pa laughed. "But there are. And they did. I've taken orders for seven fireproof coffins. Measured the sinners from toe to head. I guess they figure on hauling the boxes around with them in case of sudden need."

Finally Mr. Slathers let the cat out of the bag. I think if he'd had to wait another moment he would have exploded.

"I picked up some fresh news in Wolf Landing," he began. "Remember those two tons of dirt Shagnasty John and the Fool Killer talked about?"

"I seem to recall your mentioning it," Pa said.

"Well, it's not dirt. It's dust."

"Dust?" Ma remarked.

"*Gold* dust." Mr. Slathers leaned back and drew a long, slow puff of smoke. "Two tons of gold dust. From a rich strike last year way up in Montana. They had a terrible winter up there and the miners got froze in. The dust had been piling up and they couldn't get it out. There was a Missouri steamboat locked in the ice, but with the spring thaw the dust was put aboard for the voyage to St. Louis. With a valuable cargo like that, the captain refitted the deckhouses with tin. Word has it the job's finally done and the boat's heading downriver."

"Refitted with tin?" Ma said.

"The way they did in the Civil War, m'am. Made tin-clads out of their common riverboats. Why, every outlaw in the territories is figuring to bushwack the vessel. There's a sheriff aboard to guard the dust."

"A tin-clad," Pa mused. "That was mighty smart of the captain."

"Doesn't surprise me a bit," Mr. Slathers smiled. He took a long pause. And then he sprung his surprise. "Rumor has it the captain's name is Tuggle. Captain Jack Tuggle."

Grandpa.

And he must already be steaming toward us down the Missouri River!

19

The Return

I KEPT a sharp eye out for distant puffs of steamboat smoke.

Pa and Mr. Slathers made money enough at the coffin trade to pay off our grocery bill. They sawed up pinewood flooring that didn't seem to fit *anywhere*. And in going through the muddle of lumber, Pa found an illustrated catalog of "Lyman Bridges Building Materials and Ready-Made Houses." There were woodcut drawings of what the finished hotel and opera house were supposed to look like.

"Mr. Slathers," Pa said with a slow shake of his head. "What we're building bears no more resemblance to these pictures than a cracker barrel does to a silk hat."

As it turned out, we weren't likely to finish the opera house or hotel or anything else in Sunrise.

For Mr. Jim Chitwood returned on horseback, pulling a small shed on two buggy wheels. And with a wave of his arm he claimed ownership to all of Sunrise.

"You're squatting on my land," he declared.

"You bandy-legged, fish-eyed pipsqueak," Pa snorted. "What in blue blazes are you talking about?"

"You're trespassing — that's what I'm talking about."

"Sir, you're batty as a jaybird."

Mr. Jim Chitwood grinned and bit off a large chaw of

black tobacco. "Them miners are trespassing, too. They got no legal right to be rooting up my gold claim."

"Your claim, is it?"

Mr. Chitwood began unhitching the little frame shed on wheels. "Didn't I hear you folks say that the river jumped? Well! Maybe all this land was filed on in Dakota, but it's now Nebraska. Your title's not worth crow bait. I've been over at the land office filing my claim, Colonel. Cost me eighteen dollars in hard cash. A house is all it takes to prove up a claim, and I'm doing that now."

"You call that doghouse a *house?*"

Mr. Chitwood squeaked out a laugh. "All the law says is you've got to have a door and a winder. Look for yourself. There's a door and a winder. Even a roof. Nothing in the law says how *big* your house has got to be. Haw! Haw!"

Pa's eyes were ablaze under the brim of his hat. "You mouse-eared small end of nothing. That's a fraud and a hoax!"

"I go by the letter of the law, Colonel. Why, many a homestead's been proved up with that very two-wheeled bitty house. Rented it from a real-estate gent. We're going to have a boomtown here, with the gold and all."

I wished I could sink into the ground for not printing up the accurate truth about Glorietta's locket. Now this sly, law-spouting rascal had pulled Sunrise right out from under us. And Grandpa coming!

"That boat of yours is sitting on my land," Mr. Jim Chitwood went on. "Welcome to stay, all of you. Of course, you'll have to pay me rent. It's only proper, Colonel."

Mr. Slathers had been standing as still and silent as the

Petrified Man. But he'd been building a head of steam, and the blast of his voice about blew Mr. Jim Chitwood's ears flat back.

"*Clear out!* And take that dratted contraption with you! *Get!* And be hasty about it! If you're still in sight ten minutes from now I'm going to fold you up so that you *fit* in that bitty house and dump the tarnacious thing in the river."

Pa shook his head. "The man has the letter of the law on his side, Mr. Slathers, if not the intention. And he doesn't have title to this land yet. If I know my law it takes thirty days to prove up a claim. We don't have to pay a cent of rent. By that time the miners will give up trying to dig out gold that isn't there. Mr. Chitwood will discover he's filed on a ghost town."

Pa strode away. We all followed. I glanced back at Mr. Chitwood. There was a smile spread all over his shifty-eyed face. He'd got the best of us, and I hated him.

Glorietta climbed to the pilothouse. I was standing at the window, not far from the Great and Only Genuine Petrified Man, and watching over the treetops for black smoke. That would be Grandpa's tin-clad riverboat.

"We could hang a door and a window in the hotel," Glorietta said. "We could pay the filing fee with our buffalo-bone money. Soon as we get it."

"Where's your head, Glorietta?" I answered. "That would be jumping Mr. Chitwood's claim."

"He jumped Grandpa's!"

"But he did it legal."

"Humbug legal."

122

I nodded dismally. "Maybe Pa will take out after him and the land office and all in our newspaper. But you heard what he said. Thirty days and we'll have to pull foot for somewhere else."

"I don't want to go somewhere else. Neither does Ma."

I looked down at the new owner of Sunrise. He had unrolled a canvas sign and was hanging it on the two-wheeled shed.

SUNRISE LAND
OFFICE
prime lots for sale
Honest Jim Chilwood
Owner & Agent

I read it off and simmered all over again. He'd brought along a small table and a bentwood chair and sat himself down to wait for the land rush to start.

"Wiley!"

I turned back to Glorietta. She was staring out the window.

"I see it!" she declared in a sudden fuss of excitement.

"See what, Glorietta? You're not even wearing your specs."

"Smoke. Way upriver!"

"Imagination," I said. "Put on your specs and look again."

"I don't need to. Puffs of black smoke out there. See for yourself."

I flashed a look over the treetops. A thunderbolt couldn't have surprised me more. Maybe Glorietta was outgrowing her specs. There was smoke way off. Clear as you please!

"Grandpa's tin-clad boat," she exclaimed.

"Must be. Come on!"

We flew down the stairway and yelled for Ma and Pa. But not even Mr. Slathers was around. Maybe they were off somewhere stomping off their anger.

Glorietta and I ran like quarter horses until we reached the Missouri. We watched the black smoke unraveling in the wind and coming closer all the time. Finally we saw the top of the smokestack gliding above the tops of the trees and then we could hear the clanking of machinery and the splash of the paddle wheel.

"There it is!" I shouted.

The boat came steaming around a bend. It wasn't tin-clad. It was a trampish-looking boat, and Glorietta and I recognized it at first sight.

It was the *Prairie Buzzard* returning. Captain Cully's scruffy fertilizer boat.

Two men were standing at the jack staff waiting with ropes to jump ashore and tie up.

Suddenly we recognized them too.

Shagnasty John and the Fool Killer.

20

The Chain

THE *Prairie Buzzard* steamed right past our hill of buffalo bones and tied up in the shade of the stout old mulberry tree.

Shagnasty John saw us, tipped his hat, and gave us a broad wink. The Fool Killer hardly gave us a shrug. They wore a change of clothes, both of them — black frock coats down to their knees, stiff soiled collars, and black string ties. *The Humbug Mountain Hoorah* had hung and buried them, and now they were trying to appear respectable. But there was no changing the shifty meanness of their faces.

Captain Cully stuck his head out of the pilothouse window. "Howdy, you two," he called out, tossing us a pale-eyed smile to go with it. "How's everything in Sunrise?"

"We've got a heap of bones to sell you," I answered.

"Must be two tons," Glorietta announced. "Maybe more."

"I noticed," Captain Cully replied. "But can't use 'em."

"What?" I said.

"See for yourself. There's not so much as a chicken bone aboard. I've retired from the fertilizer trade."

126

Glorietta and I exchanged quick looks. We'd about broken our backs toting gunnysack loads. But it was true — the decks of the *Prairie Buzzard* were bare. All I saw was a huge iron anchor chain piled near the bow. Each link looked big as a wagon hub.

"But you promised!" Glorietta said, coming to a quick boil.

"My dear friends," Captain Cully replied in a prayer-meeting tone of voice. "Me and my new partners have gone into the trade of saving souls. Say hello to the Reverend Mr. Chubb and the Reverend Mr. Shoeless Harry Dunster."

"Bless you, young'uns," said Shagnasty John, who had refitted himself with the name of Chubb. The Fool Killer stared at us with his deep, hellfire eyes as if warning us to keep our mouths shut.

That tarnacious pair had pulled the wool over Captain Cully's eyes. It surprised me that he'd got religion so quick and sudden.

Glorietta lifted her chin. "You said you'd buy all the buffalo bones we could collect. Four dollars a ton. You promised!"

"Bless my sinner's hide, I do hate to go back on my word, little children. But the Lord's work comes first."

"We're not little children," Glorietta snapped back.

"Trust in Providence, my lambs. Another scow is bound to turn up for your cargo of bones. Now you two run along. I've got to clean the Lord's mud out of my boiler, and then we'll be moving on, doing our good works. Amen."

"Come on, Glorietta," I sputtered angrily. No doubt

about it — we were stuck with a useless pile of bones. But at least we'd soon be rid of Shagnasty John and the Fool Killer.

Then I turned my head. "Maybe you've seen a tin-clad steamboat upriver," I called back. "Know if it's close behind?"

"A tin-clad!" Captain Cully bellowed out a laugh. "Why I never heard of such a thing on the Missouri. Tin-clad, do you say? Well, that beats all."

"Just like in the Civil War," I answered, feeling challenged on the matter.

"No such boat coming. Just river gossip. Say howdy to your folks."

"The Reverend Mr. Chubb and the Reverend Mr. Shoeless Harry Dunster!" Pa roared out laughing. "Aren't those two cutthroats taking on airs? And you say Captain Cully has thrown in with them?"

"Yes, sir," I answered.

"I don't believe he's fooled at all. Saving souls! What rubbish. If they're not gone by morning they'll bear watching."

"And he won't buy our heap of bones."

It was the vision of that heap of bones that awoke me out of a sound sleep. I sat straight up. By morning Captain Cully might be gone, and our bones with him. They were there for the taking. And I didn't trust Captain Cully any farther than I could throw a barn.

I slipped out of the pilothouse and down the stairway and across the gangplank. I could see the faint glow of coals not yet died out in the campsites along the old riverbank. I cut through the cottonwoods and made a beeline for the Missouri.

Our mountain of bones was still there, white as chalk in the starlight.

I paused to catch my breath. And then voices drifted toward me from the mulberry tree. I edged closer along the bank and dropped to my stomach.

Captain Cully and his partners were wrestling an end of the heavy iron chain ashore. I watched as they secured the end around the mulberry tree.

"That ought to hold," I heard Captain Cully say.

I spent hours watching. Captain Cully started up the engine of the *Prairie Buzzard* and carefully worked the boat to the other side of the river. Shagnasty John and the Fool Killer stood at the bow feeding out the monstrous chain, link by link.

When they reached the far bank they hauled out sharpened wood stakes as big around as railroad ties. They spent an eternity swinging mauls to pound the cluster of stakes into the bank.

Shagnasty John was huffing hard, and I heard Captain Cully say, "Keep at it, Shagnasty. We've got to get it done before daylight."

Well, he knew who Shagnasty John was all along.

It was near daylight when they finished. I knew I ought to slip away. I reckoned they'd kill me if they knew I was watching. But I couldn't tear myself away until I figured out what they were up to.

They lugged the chain around and around the tight cluster of stakes and locked the end in place with a couple of crowbars. Then they shoveled dirt to cover the chain.

In the pale dawn light I saw they had drawn the chain like an iron fence from bank to bank across the river. They'd set it so that not a link showed above the surface of the muddy water.

I scuttled backward and out of their sight. Grandpa's tin-clad must be close behind after all, I thought. A cold sweat shot out over me. He wouldn't see the chain, and he'd go crashing into it. Shagnasty John and the Fool Killer meant to board the boat like pirates and the *Prairie Buzzard* would make off with that two tons of gold dust!

I didn't dare get to my feet and run. They'd see me. I crawled away through the dirt and weeds. Pa and Mr. Slathers would know what to do!

I never remembered the sun to rise so fast. I kept rushing along, pausing once for a quick glance over my shoulder. I could still see the *Prairie Buzzard* bigger'n life.

And then I heard it. The blast of a steamboat whistle. Upriver.

The hair on my neck stiffened. I got to my knees, but there wasn't going to be time enough to run for Pa.

I could already see puffs of smoke and sparks in the sky. And then a silver boat flashed through the upriver cottonwoods. It gave off sunlight like a distant mirror.

Grandpa's tin-clad, for sure.

21

The Tin-clad

CROWS WERE PERCHED on the hill of buffalo bones. They went squawking into the air as I climbed to the top. I had to keep Grandpa from charging into the mighty iron chain stretched from bank to bank.

"Wiley! Fool Killer!"

I pulled off my shirt. The tin-clad steamed around bends and oxbows, flashing and drawing nearer and closer. Shagnasty John and the Fool Killer could use me for a shooting target, for all I cared.

I got ready to wave my shirt. I wished it were red. That would warn Grandpa of trouble ahead. But it was only the color of oatmeal mush. It would have to do, and I'd yell myself hoarse.

I caught sight of the miners fleeing out of the old riverbed as if they'd dug up the devil red-hot from home. Gold pans, picks, shovels, and bedrolls flew over the bank. I had no idea what was wrong and no time to wonder about it. The blast of the tin-clad's whistle sounded through the trees.

Grandpa wasn't likely to hear me yell over the whistling and the chugging of the engine. And with two tons of gold dust aboard he might not even slow down for a shirttail boy waving a mush-colored shirt.

Off to my left, the miners' voices were rising in shouts. "Run for your lives!"

"Get to high ground!"

"Dad-bob fools! They burrowed in smack through to the Missouri. *And here it comes!*"

I couldn't help looking. I saw a muddy gush of water breaking away from the channel. The miners were climbing the river bluff like ants. And then the earth itself seemed to bust apart. Great sections of the bank collapsed with a tumbling roar. A sheet of water went rushing along the dry diggings. Tree stumps and logs leaped into the air and raced away a mile a minute.

My eyes almost stood out of my head. The Missouri was jumping its banks again.

And jumping right back into its old riverbed!

A long blast of the steamboat whistle brought me around. The tall smokestack above the treetops didn't appear more than a half mile off.

My heart was thumping like a donkey engine. I began waving my shirt. The heap of buffalo bones was sure to catch Grandpa's eye, I told myself. And it wasn't every day you saw a boy waving a shirt on a heap of buffalo bones. Maybe it was enough to make him pause and wonder. Slow down, at least!

The shirt was snatched out of my hands so quick it appeared to vanish in midair. I spun around and there stood the Fool Killer, taller'n a tree, and with his bur-oak club resting on a shoulder. He tossed my shirt aside.

"I catched me a fool," he said, and his eyes burned madly in their hollows. "I smite fools with my club. That's my trade."

"You're gone-minded," I declared. "There's no such real thing as the Fool Killer!"

He raised the club in both hands to bring it thundering down on my skull. He swung and I dodged clear. He swung again and I scuttled to the other side. Neither of us could get a good foothold on all those buffalo ribs and skulls.

I could hear the thump and splash of Grandpa's boat behind me, but I didn't dare look. The Fool Killer tracked me around the top of the bone heap and swung again. I got my hands on a buffalo rib and flung it at him.

That put him in such a hopping rage that he came at me circling the club with so much might it almost whistled. But he forgot his footing and the mess of bones tangled his left foot. I'd already picked up another rib, but I didn't need to throw it. The bur-oak club had so much swing left in it that it caught the rear of his own skull. He went sprawling down. The Fool Killer had *catched* himself.

I snatched up my shirt and turned as the silvery boat was clearing the nearest bend, dead ahead. It was so close I could see a man at the pilothouse wheel. He was peering through the open window. A long cigar between his teeth was clamped at a devil-may-care angle under the bill of his black cap.

I waved the shirt and began yelling: "Grandpa! Captain! Grandpa!"

Maybe he saw me. But something else caught his eye. Between us the Missouri River was roaring lickety-cut down its old bed, and draining the new.

Grandpa cocked his head a moment and then spun the spokes of the big steering wheel into a blur.

The tin-clad was turning! The bobtailed paddle wheel

swung into view. Grandpa was following the fresh flow of water. He was steering into the old riverbed!

Wild relief almost lifted me off my feet. The Fool Killer turned himself over with a groan. He was going to have a headache fit for a mule. I glanced over at the *Prairie Buzzard*. The river had already dropped so low the chain had come into clear view. In no time at all Captain Cully's boat would be sitting sunk and dry on the bottom!

I scrambled down the bone heap and ran.

22

Quickshot Billy

THE *Phoenix* was afloat!

She had been lifted from the river bottom as if from a dusty grave, and her old mooring lines had held. By the time I came charging along, Grandpa's tin-clad was giving off merry blasts of her whistle as her paddle wheel splashed in reverse. She was mooring along the bluff just behind the *Phoenix.*

Ma was all smiles. Her eyes drifted back to the *Phoenix.* "Sits on the water pretty as a duck, doesn't she?"

Pa stood watching, and so did the bandy-legged, mouse-eared landowner of Sunrise. "Mr. Chitwood," Pa said, without even favoring the man with a glance. "Roll up your sign, hitch up your pipsqueak house, and make tracks out of here. Your Nebraska title is not worth crow bait. The river has jumped your claim, sir. This is Dakota Territory again. You're trespassing." Mr. Jim Chitwood went slinking off like a rained-on dog.

The tin-clad shut down its engine, and Grandpa stepped out of the pilothouse.

The sight of the *Phoenix* kindled a twinkle in his eyes. Then he took a jaunty look at the half-built hotel, the half-built opera house, Mr. Johnson running loose, and the entire population of Sunrise. He took the cigar out of his mouth and said, "What in Sam Hill's going on here?"

Miners were gathering around for a look at the tin-clad boat, and he didn't see Ma at first. "Is that you, Mr. Slathers?"

"It is, Captain."

"You still here!"

"Ain't left! And look at the *Phoenix*. Greased and oiled and even the doorknobs polished. Waiting for you, Captain."

"I declare!"

Then he spied Ma in the crowd. He lifted his cap, gave a wave, stepped lively down the ladder, and jumped ashore.

"Jenny!"

"Welcome to Sunrise, Father," Ma exclaimed. "Welcome home!"

He opened his arms and snugged her to him.

Then he shook Pa's hand. But he didn't recognize Glorietta, and he didn't recognize me. I suddenly realized we were strangers.

"Father," Ma said, and turned him to face us.

"Glorietta?" he enquired, in a kind of awe. "Wiley!"

We both stood there in a fit of shyness.

He tossed away his cigar. The next thing Glorietta knew she was hoisted high in the air. He kissed her cheek and looked at me. He calculated I was too old for that kind of thing, and shot out his hand.

I shook it. His hand was huge and rough, but friendly.

"By ginger! Haven't you both sprouted up!"

I stood there wishing I were at *least* as sprouted up as Glorietta. I was older and it wasn't fair. There was no rushing a matter like getting your full height, hang it all! I'd just have to wait. But he *had* shook my hand as if I were a grown-up.

"So you're the first lady pilot on the Missouri," Grandpa said. "And Wiley, didn't I read that you are sheriff around here?"

"That was just make-believe, Grandpa."

"Well, what's this I heard in Wolf Landing about a Petrified Man?"

"I was the first to find it, Grandpa!" Glorietta said. "If you don't count Mr. Johnson. He's only Ma's goose. And I wasn't even wearing my glasses. I've outgrown them."

"I declare. And what's this about a gold strike in Sunrise?"

I had to clear my throat. "That was my doing," I confessed. "I didn't know it was going to cause such a fuss to leave out a word. All Ma found in the chicken craw was the gold locket you gave Glorietta."

Grandpa laughed, and tipped back his captain's cap. "Not the first time men have run gold fever on a wisp of bobtailed nothing! And they'll stampede after the next rumor that comes along. Shoveled up a storm, did they?"

"Yes, sir," I said.

"Healthful exercise. I'm obliged to them. It appears to me the word you left out refloated the *Phoenix*." And then he narrowed one eye. "Was that you standing on a bone pile waving your shirt?"

I told him about the goings-on aboard the *Prairie Buzzard.*

"A chain across the river! Well, well. That took cast-iron grit to stand up there. I'm proud of you, Wiley."

I glowed up inside, but tried not to let it show. I certainly didn't feel that we were strangers anymore.

He turned and gave a shout to the tin-clad. "Quickshot! Come out here and meet a fellow lawman!"

"Quickshot?" I said. "Not Quickshot Billy Bodeen? — Scourge of the Western Badmen?"

"The same. Hired him on to protect our cargo. Outlaws have been banging away at us like a tin can all the way down the river. See all the bullet holes? The boat owner couldn't find any fool but me to make the run. And Marshal Bodeen. But he's so gun-shy he's afraid to poke his head out. Lost his nerve."

Quickshot Billy afraid? That was impossible! Quickshot Billy had nerves of steel.

"Marshal! Stop hiding and come here, confound you!"

A tin-clad door opened and my breath about choked with awe. There he stood. Quickshot Billy Bodeen in person.

He wore a big white Stetson hat, just like he wore in the book pictures, but his legs were so bowed you could run a hog through them. And you could hardly see his gunbelt for his stomach hanging out over it. He looked as blown up as a colicky horse. I wondered how he located his guns for his famous quick draw.

His eyes shifted from side to side, taking us all in, and then he straightened back his shoulders and pulled the Stetson sharply over his eyes.

"I'm ready for trouble, Captain," he declared.

"No trouble. I've got a grandson here and he's the duly

appointed sheriff of Sunrise. According to the papers, he captured Shagnasty John and the Fool Killer single-handed."

I felt my face heat up, red with embarrassment.

"Kind of pint-sized for a lawman, ain't he?"

"Full of cast-iron grit, though," Grandpa answered.

"I've read your books of true adventures," I managed to say. "I've even got a mirror ring just like yours."

"A mirror ring? What the deuce is that?"

Didn't he know? I guessed those nickel novels stretched the truth here and there, but I tried hard to fight off the crush of disappointment. Maybe Quickshot Billy was running slightly to tallow, but he must have once been tall and lean and scared of no man.

As I gazed at him he was doing his best to hold back his stomach and look cool-eyed and fearless behind the badge on his shirt. I filled with a kind of sadness. I felt sorry for him.

Suddenly his eyes lit up as if he'd spied an old friend. "I'll be hanged! If it ain't Colonel Flint!"

My eyes flashed up at Pa. His face went kind of white under his knife-brim hat. I'd never seen him look so flustered. "Hello, Quickshot," he muttered.

I could hardly believe my hearing. Pa had never let on that he knew Quickshot Billy Bodeen.

"Colonel, those are bully fine stories you wrote about me," the marshal said. "Reckon there must be some ain't come my way. Durned if I recall wearing a mirror on my finger ring."

I gazed at Pa, thunderstruck. Had *he* written those nickel novels I toted around? Why had he kept it such a

140

dark, tightfisted secret? Pa's eyes looked everywhere but at me. He was fidgety with embarrassment.

The marshal tried to hitch up his gunbelt. "I'm powerfully disappointed that Shagnasty John and the Fool Killer's been caught and buried," he was saying. "Wanted the pleasure of capturing them myself."

"You may have the chance," Grandpa said. "Those two have popped up out of their graves."

"And here we are!"

The voice came bellowing out through the crowd. Crows in the treetops began squawking.

"Shagnasty John!"

"The Fool Killer!"

In the lead came Shagnasty John with a gun in each hand. The Fool Killer followed, toting his bur-oak club and rifle, his head wrapped in a dirty rag. There was a look in his eyes as if he still couldn't see straight.

"Reach up your hands! Every man jack!" Shagnasty John snarled.

Arms went into the air, stiff as fence pickets.

"That includes you, Colonel! Don't go for your pepperbox!"

I looked at Quickshot Billy. He was reaching for the sky like everybody else!

"No one'll get hurt," said Shagnasty John, offering up a grin through his dirt-brown beard. "We just mean to change the ownership of that tin-clad boat. A simple business transaction. Our pilot'll be along soon as we finish negotiatin'." And then he noticed the marshal's badge on Quickshot Billy's shirt.

He snorted out a laugh. "Fool Killer, see what we got here!"

"What?"

"The genuine law. Marshal, lower your cussed arms and draw. We don't want a tin-star on our tracks again."

Quickshot Billy kept his hands in the air.

"I said draw! That's your job, ain't it?"

I saw all the color fade out of Quickshot Billy's face.

"You deaf, Marshal? Drop your arms and go for your guns!"

Quickshot Billy looked stunned. He only gazed at them.

"Cuss it all, Marshal. I got just so much patience. I'll have to shoot you as you stand."

Shagnasty raised both guns and took aim with the pair of them.

The breath was caught in my throat. Quickshot Billy stood frozen. I recollected his adventures with the chili peppers. I twisted my mirror ring. I caught the sun in it and squirted the reflection smack into Shagnasty John's eyes. He fired.

The shots went so wild they shattered a window in the pilothouse of the *Phoenix*. The Fool Killer commenced blasting away too, but he was so perishing gone-minded now he seemed overjoyed just to raise a clanging from the tin-clad. Mr. Johnson started honking and flapping his wings and running about in a fright. The Fool Killer's attention strayed. He dropped the rifle and took off after the goose, flailing away with his club.

I kept the sunlight dancing in Shagnasty John's eyes. He tried to brush it away like a pesky fly. All the ruckus seemed to scare some of the fear out of Quickshot Billy.

I saw him fumbling around for his guns. His draw wasn't exactly quicker'n the eye, but he did take careful aim.

A puff of smoke shot out of the barrel. Shagnasty John's hat flew off his head. "Fool Killer! I've gone sun blind! Finish him off!"

"Drop your irons!" Quickshot Billy roared. "You're under arrest."

"Fool Killer!"

"Raise your hands!"

"Fool Killer!"

"He's off chasing a goose," said the marshal. He paused, arms akimbo. "No, by gum, now the goose is chasing him."

Shagnasty John gave out a great, bellowing groan and dropped his guns.

Quickshot Billy must have been carrying a ton of manacles aboard the tin-clad, and before long Shagnasty John and the Fool Killer seemed to be wearing them all. The marshal said he'd turn the men and hardware over to the law in St. Louis.

He sauntered about with a strong, silent look on his face. But I knew he'd never be the Quickshot Billy I'd imagined, and I reckoned he never was. I guessed he'd never squirted a chili pepper at real outlaws. Pa must have whipped up those adventures out of his own head. But that was all right. Glorietta had outgrown her specs and I figured I'd outgrown pretending I had a close friend in those dog-eared nickel novels.

I found myself standing in Quickshot Billy's monstrous shadow. He gave me a wink. "Let me see that looking-glass ring, Wiley," he said. "Wish I had me one of those confounded things."

144

23

The Secret

"IT'S A DAD-BLASTED FAKE," Grandpa laughed. "It's a humbug!"

We had all followed along as he inspected the *Phoenix* and pronounced it mostly fit. When we reached the pilot-house, we saw that Shagnasty John's wild shots through the window had knocked off the whole left thumb of the Great and Only Genuine Petrified Man.

"No bone in the hand," said Grandpa. "Not a splinter. The petrified gent was hand-chiseled out of solid lime-stone."

"Well, the laugh is certainly on us," Ma said.

Pa was awfully quiet. His eyes avoided Glorietta and me. Ever since Quickshot Billy had exposed him as the writer of his daring exploits and adventures, Pa looked as if he wanted to climb under a flat rock and hide. I didn't understand why he was so dang sheepish about it.

"Someone must have planned on digging up the con-founded statue after properly aging it," Grandpa said. "Might have been able to swindle a circus or museum out of a princely sum of money for it."

Ma turned to Pa. "Rufus, we'll be obliged to put out another edition of the paper exposing the hoax."

"Of course," Pa answered, but he hardly seemed to be listening.

"Why, Colonel, just move it to the opera house and charge ten cents admission," Grandpa said. "There's so little to see out here folks will come a long way to look at a genuine hoax!" He was gazing at the empty lots of Sunrise. "We'll put a general store down there. Schoolhouse up there. With the river jumped back, saloons will spring up like weeds. I'd better bring back lumber for a church." He cocked his head. "But that pile of buffalo bones is an eyesore."

"Dreadful eyesore," Glorietta agreed.

"I'll haul 'em off to the factory soon as I'm back at the wheel of the *Phoenix*. What'll you take for 'em?"

"Captain Cully said four dollars a ton," I said.

"Why, the dishonest, mildewed cheat! They'll fetch twice that. Sold — for eight dollars a ton!"

I remained behind in the pilothouse. With the boat lifted by the river, I could now see over the treetops. I tried to imagine Sunrise all built up, the way it appeared in our rolled-up color lithograph. Glorietta and I would have heaps of our own friends before long, I thought. Heaps. Unless Pa was coming down with the yonders again. I didn't know what to think.

The crows caught my eye. They were flocked in the distance like flecks of pepper over the stranded and done-for *Prairie Buzzard*. It seemed to me I could make out Captain Cully himself. He was digging a hole at a fierce rate. Shovel dirt was flying.

I watched him a long time. It was *Captain Cully* who

had buried the humbug Petrified Man! No doubt about it. He was digging in the very spot.

Grandpa chuckled. "It was you, was it, Colonel, who wrote up those grandacious lies about Quickshot Billy! I don't mind confessing he was hired on the strength of the bully reputation you gave him. Good reading, those yarns."

"Confounded trash," Pa snapped. "I regard myself as both a newspaperman and a serious man of letters, Captain. A poet. Those nickel novels are an intense embarrassment. But from time to time we needed money."

"Rufus," Ma sighed, and then gave her head a toss. "I don't know how much longer I could have kept your secret. You're a splendid poet and you must get on with your new book. But you've got more pride than a *roomful* of poets."

"Pa, I *liked* those stories," I said. "Is that what you were doing over in Wolf Landing? When you locked yourself in the hotel room? Were you writing another story?"

Pa hesitated. Then he gave a small shrug. *"Quickshot Billy, Whirlwind of the West."*

"Well, I hope you put some girls in it this time, Pa," Glorietta said.

Pa's eyes settled on us for the first time. "It was hard on you the way I'd disappear. I know that."

Glorietta stood mum, staring at Pa. So did I, thinking back.

Pa said softly, "I may have kept a secret, but I've never lied to you. When our money ran low I had no choice but to lock myself away in order to scribble out that nonsense. Around the clock, for days and sometimes weeks, in secret.

147

I wrote under a dozen different names." He took a long breath. "Hang it all, I not only made Quickshot Billy's reputation, but one for myself — *King of the Nickel Novels!*"

My eyebrows rose. "Honest?" I exclaimed. I thought it sounded glorious!

Pa looked from one of us to the other. He appeared confounded that we weren't embarrassed to have a father who was King of the Nickel Novels.

"Then you won't have to disappear again, will you, Pa?" Glorietta said.

Pa's eyes slid to Ma. "Jenny, do you have that catalog of Lyman Bridges Ready-Made Houses? Study it over and pick out a home to your liking."

"I already have. House Number 27. It has a lovely parlor with a bay window, and three bedrooms and the prettiest front porch."

Pa withdrew an envelope from his pocket. It was the letter Mr. Slathers had brought back from Wolf Landing. "Captain, this is a check from my publisher. When you return with the general store, the schoolhouse, and the church, will you kindly bring us House Number 27?"

It was late morning when Grandpa boarded the tin-clad to leave. But then he turned to Pa. "I'm afraid those asbestos coffins you advertised will draw a rough brand of citizen, Colonel."

"It takes all kinds to make a town, Captain," said Pa.

"I think we're going to need a sheriff to handle the sinners who show up."

"You're not thinking of Quickshot Billy?" Glorietta said with a faint groan.

I found myself standing up for him. "He did get back his nerve at the last minute, Glorietta."

"Appears to be an ounce or two of grit in him," Grandpa said. "I'll confess, it surprised me."

And Ma said, "We'll get busy on the next issue of *The Humbug Mountain Hoorah*. Didn't he save two tons of gold dust and capture two notorious outlaws?"

Pa gave me a wink. "With Wiley's help. Oh, Quickshot will walk the streets of Sunrise with such a strong reputation that ruffians will run like rabbits at the sight of him."

Grandpa gave us a wave, and before long the tin-clad was churning out of sight downriver.

I looked at the mirror ring on my finger. I'd give it to Quickshot Billy Bodeen. He might need all the help he could get.